Praise for An Une:

"Lovers of Greek myths and myth retellings should not miss this soaring tale. With *An Unexpected Ally*, Sophia Kouidou-Giles takes the oft-maligned goddess of sorcery to new heights and dimensions. In this fresh take, love, hate, and jealousy are channeled into a compelling story of sisterhood."

—MARIA A. KARAMITSOS, author, former publisher, and founder of *WindyCity Greek* magazine

"Kouidou-Giles's book captivates the reader from the first paragraph. The story traveled me to vibrant worlds with rich descriptions of an ancient, mythical world. Through the fascinating adventures of Circe, the author extols the talents, emotions, and skills of the feminine nature, revealing the primary virtues of female solidarity. A page-turner!"

—NORA KAZAZI, author of *Colours of My Soul* (Στα Χρώματα της Ψυχής Μου)

"*An Unexpected Ally* is an enchanted reimagining of an ancient Greek myth and has all the hallmarks of human drama with a powerful woman, Circe, at the center of the story. Circe includes timeless themes of family conflict, use and misuse of power, desire, prophecy, dreams, sacrifices to the gods, and love gone awry. Curl up in front of the fire or enjoy this book sitting in the sun on vacation. A fun and educational read, *An Unexpected Ally* is highly recommended."

—DIANA ENGLISH, PhD, author of *The Well of Sorrow*

"What a wonderful mix of adventure, mythology, and age-old relationship issues; the reader encounters engaging, unusual characters and visual images that take them out of the daily grind and into another realm, including under the sea and into the sky. A true adventure tale with just enough history and psychology to elevate it above mere escapist pleasure."

—MARY WEIKERT, journalist and author

"What an unexpected retelling, filled with characters from Greek mythology! It's an enjoyable read with twists and turns!"

—MEG MAHONEY, contributing writer
to the *Baltimore Review* and the *Lumiere Review*

AN
UNEXPECTED
ALLY

A GREEK TALE OF LOVE, REVENGE, AND REDEMPTION

SOPHIA KOUIDOU-GILES

SHE WRITES PRESS

Published 2023

Printed in the United States of America

Print ISBN: 978-1-64742-555-5
E-ISBN: 978-1-64742-556-2
Library of Congress Control Number: 2023907749

For information, address:
She Writes Press
1569 Solano Ave #546
Berkeley, CA 94707

Interior design and layout by Katherine Lloyd, The DESK

She Writes Press is a division of SparkPoint Studio, LLC.

This is a work of fiction. Names, characters, places, and incidents either are the product of the author's imagination or are used fictitiously. Any resemblance to actual persons, living or dead, is entirely coincidental.

To my grandsons, Oscar and Damon,
who love mythology.

With love,
Yiayia

"You had the power all along, my dear."
—Glinda the Good Witch
in *The Wizard of Oz* by L. Frank Baum

PART I

They reached the gates of the goddess's house, and as they stood there they could hear Circe within, singing most beautifully as she worked at her loom, making a web so fine, so soft, and of such dazzling colours as no one but a goddess could weave. On this Polites, whom I valued and trusted more than any other of my men, said, "There is someone inside working at a loom and singing most beautifully; the whole place resounds with it, let us call her and see whether she is woman or goddess."

—Homer, *The Odyssey*: Book 10.240–5
[*The Odyssey* (Trans. Samuel Butler)]

ONE

"How do we know the ones we love? Do we? Do we really love them, or are they companions for a time?" Circe was in one of her moods. She was working on another tapestry, chatting with her faithful servant, Melis.

"Mistress," Melis offered, wringing her hands. "All you have to do is choose your man. Who can resist you? Who has ever resisted you before?"

The all-knowing enchantress smiled to herself, for she saw her servant was trying to lift her out of her melancholy. Pointing to the tangled-up spools and threads stacked by the wall, she ordered, "Sort by color." Melis rolled up her sleeves and followed instructions.

For an instant, immortal Circe believed Melis's words. She could conquer him, this creature she had recently seen in her dreams. He might be a good prospect to follow Odysseus, a man who was no longer in love with her but who had stolen her heart. There had been times she thought of keeping him, slipping him a potion, forcing him to stay, but then she would kill what she loved about him, his moxie, his willpower, his independence. She did not want to keep him tamed, a creature bent to her will.

Melis fastened her black bandana around her graying hair and bent down to collect what had fallen on the floor. "Odysseus is homesick," she mumbled.

Circe only glanced toward her servant before returning to her own thoughts. Despite her affection for the cunning warrior, the enchantress was almost ready to release him. "He deserves his fate: meandering the seas in search of Ithaca," she declared with a smirk.

Melis's eyes lit up. "Maybe it's time . . . but you will have no trouble finding another." After all, to beguile and allure were part and parcel of Circe's charms; she rarely needed to use her incantations in matters of the heart.

Circe, the daughter of Helios, the mighty Titan, and the ocean nymph Perse, left her loom and picked up her golden mirror. A pair of wide-set blue-green eyes stared back from a young woman's face, the hair parted with a fine bone comb and tossed to the right. Her skin was smooth and supple. Her chin was pointed, the mark of a decisive woman. Her voluptuous lips tempted every man she ever wanted to pair up with. She touched up her hair. *That's better*, she thought, and smiled, satisfied.

The goddess felt Melis's gaze follow her. Circe had confided to her that the newest object of her curiosity was exotic, fascinating, immortal, a creature of the land and the sea. Like her, he had a deep knowledge of herbs and the gift of prophecy; that made him an equal, an intriguing first for a partner. His name was Glaucus. He had been transformed from an everyday fishmonger to an amphibian god, or so she had heard from Odysseus's crew.

When the servant finished tidying up, she excused herself. Alone again, Circe walked over to her collection of threads and fabrics. She chose a couple of skeins of blue thread and took them to the loom, but she was done working for the day. Over the eons, she had tired from so many losses. However, she could not quiet her thoughts. Could this god be who she hoped for, an immortal companion for an immortal sorceress? Immortality was not all it was cracked up to be. She definitely wanted to have a hand in shaping her own fortune. But life could be unpredictable; there were complicated alliances between Olympian gods and humans. Tides often shifted; she had been caught in those eddies herself from time to time.

On her way to the kitchen, in a swirl of confusion, Melis was puzzling about her lady's plight. She knew Circe to be a powerful woman who did not trust people and relied on her own instincts about things. Her mistress was lonely and chose her lovers well—but an amphibian? What would that be like? Odysseus had come, stayed for a year, and would soon be gone. She knew he was the only one ever to abandon her mistress. That must smart.

Melis did not keep Circe's confidences to herself. She stopped to taste some figs the girls had plucked from an overloaded tree, so ripe they were dripping honey, and shared the news. "Circe is interested in an amphibian god. She has been asking questions, gathering every tidbit she can from Odysseus himself and his men," she said, with a smug smile. All ears perked up and soon it was the whisper of the day. "They come and they go . . . They come and they go . . ."

Some had sympathy. "She is upset. Odysseus is leaving her," said the washerwoman, still scrubbing pots and pans.

"Give her time to get over him," added her helper.

Others were in disbelief: "Such a crazy idea." They all wondered if all the witchcraft in the world could make this relationship work. She was of the land, he of the sea.

Then the talk shifted to Circe's past affairs and lovers. Melis reminded them that any human would eventually die and leave her alone once more. The girls liked those who gave them small gifts to thank them for their services. Not everybody did. "Remember the ribbons I got?" said the pretty one.

"I remember, but he liked me better. He gave me a belt made of shells," answered the one watching the cauldron simmering over the coals.

"What would an amphibian give us?" wondered the third.

"More sea trinkets?" They giggled and started listing what they would like to receive.

"What matters most is what Circe gives you, girls," said Melis, who had fed the gossip but did not care for their greed and squabbles.

Earlier in the week on a particular evening, Circe's servers had been waiting for her to take her place next to Odysseus at the table and begin dining as they did every night. She was late. As she rushed along the halls, her gauzy tunic fanning out behind her, she had not yet settled on a plan of action. That afternoon, roaming alone in the forest, she had debated whether to grant Odysseus's plea to release him. Her steps had taken her to the uncovered pigsty where his men, still in pig form as they'd been since the day she'd first cast her spell, were guttling the roots and greens her slave girls had poured into the troughs.

Invisible, she rested on a fallen tree trunk behind some tall palm trees and listened to their conversation. "We'll never see Ithaca again," a couple of them mourned, rolling in the mud to cool down from the hot day. After a year in the pigsty, even hardened warriors were giving up hope. Circe knew she held their fortunes.

Elpinikis, one of Odysseus's lead men, spoke up. "Odysseus will convince Circe to let us leave her island and return home to Ithaca." He walked around the pen looking at each sailor in the eye: "Remember the prophecy Glaucus gave us. We *will* get away. Odysseus is crafty and soon we'll board our ship. We have overcome so many obstacles. Glaucus told us we would see our home again."

Circe's ears perked up. It was the first time she heard of Glaucus. Who might that be? She approached the pigsty, staying a few feet away from the muddy ground, and called Elpinikis by his name.

"Who is this Glaucus?"

Surprised, the white swine moved closer to the sorceress, making his voice humble: "What do you want to know, mighty Circe?"

"What did he prophesy?" Her eyes narrowed. "Who and where is he?"

Despite his piggish form, she saw that the young man was reluctant to share much. "He was an everyday fishmonger, my goddess," he tried, laconic as ever. "But now he is immortal: a god, with the divine gift of prophecy. He gave us hope we will return home someday."

"Where did you meet him?" she asked, tilting her head.

"In Delos, when we all swam in the calm waters of that bay."

"Is he really a god?" she persisted, intrigued by the unexpected information.

"That is what Odysseus said. Ask him," Elpinikis answered, moving away and lowering his head to get a drink of water. Circe read his mind, felt his fear, and sensed his yearning to see her notorious magic wand that had transformed kings and slaves alike. She knew he would never beg for what he most wanted: for her to shift them back to their old selves.

Noticing the setting sun, Circe realized she was holding up dinner. She rushed away, following a path inhabited by birds she had transformed from human enemies. They chirped pleasing songs to the enchantress.

Up ahead, she could see that her servers had already set the table for two. She and Odysseus met there every night no matter where their day took them. Odysseus, the king of Ithaca and leader of men, had been repairing the ship, moored on the bay. A short man, dark-skinned and muscular, with small dark eyes and an unkempt beard, he liked working with his rough hands. Circe tracked his progress. By now he had most everything in good shape. She knew he worried about her delaying their departure. To watch him, though, sipping wine diluted with water from the wide-mouthed cylix that the slave girls kept refilling for him, no one would know he was fretting. It was time for the biggest meal of the day, and he would be hungry. Circe moved so silently that no one could hear the pitter-patter of her feet, and she took her seat across from him without an apology. "Have you kept busy today?"

Looking surprised, he swallowed a bite of cheese and reached for a fig. "Busy making some last repairs to the ship. My sailors and I are ready to leave. Another day when home is calling, Circe." The pleading in his eyes forced her to recognize that their affair had to be over soon. She had promised him she would return his men to their human form when the time came.

In a sharp, almost accusing tone, she said, "You have some guidance from Glaucus for your trip back home, I understand. You have never mentioned him. Is he credible?"

She refilled his cylix herself and watched Odysseus take a moment, thoughtful, staring at the image drawn on the bottom of it: Apollo wearing a laurel wreath on his head. She smiled to herself, noticing the king of Ithaca's surprise that she was aware of Glaucus. "Is he a man or an immortal god?" she pressed.

"A god," he answered carefully. "Beautiful and unusual, he shifted in form from human to an amphibian creature, growing fins instead of arms and a fish tail instead of legs. He knows about life's mysteries and has the gift of prophecy."

Circe motioned for Odysseus to go on.

"He certainly knows a lot about herbs. Many go to Delos to ask him about the future."

"What else do you know?" Her eyes stayed on him.

"Nothing more." He shrugged. "Some gods want to see us back home and others don't. He was sympathetic." He took a breath and looked away from her. "But where is our meal?"

She snapped her fingers to signal to the servers that they were ready for more food. They rushed in a platter with fish and asparagus and they filled their plates, eating until Circe complained to the slaves. "Wait until we have come to the table before you steam the fish. It's cold. I can barely eat it." She knew it was her own fault for being late. Still, they were there to serve them perfect meals.

They finished with a handful of ripe, delicious figs Circe had ordered her maids to gather from the garden. Not ready to call it a night, and since the evening was mellow, they moved to the patio where Odysseus told stories about a couple of constellations that he knew well from navigating the seas. Shifting his weight from one foot to the other, he pointed to the Pleiades, the six sisters Zeus had turned to pigeons and sent to the night sky to shine like diamonds and help sailors find their way. Close to them was amorous Orion, son of Poseidon, a hunter in pursuit of the sisters. Odysseus had a charming way with words and Circe enjoyed his illuminating stories, but it was getting late and the couple withdrew to their bedroom.

That night Apollo, the lord of Delos, who was fond of the enchantress, sent Circe a vivid dream. He and the other Olympians watched and interfered in her affairs from time to time. The image was of a man rowing his boat out to sea. The man was tall, with long hair that danced in the breeze. His youthful face glowed under the rays of a full moon. He set his rod to the bottom of his boat, dropped anchor, and baited his fishing hook. Circe's gaze sank under the surface of a sapphire sea, discerning the form of a woman who looked familiar; it was her mother, Perse, the ocean nymph, her braided black hair coming loose as she approached Glaucus's boat. She took the fishing hook dangling in the water and forced a fish to swallow it. Then she stood by to watch what the fishmonger would do. Sensing the pull on his line, the man netted the fish and was about to drop it into his bucket but hesitated. He held it for an instant, as though feeling its life quivering away, then released it back to the salty sea, delivering it back to life. With a look of relief on his face, he dipped his oars into the water and steered his vessel to shore.

The dream jarred Circe awake. She did not wake Odysseus. Her mind was racing. It was rare to see her mother in her dreams. The two women were not close and Perse's relationship with Helios was everything Circe was afraid of, a conflicted, humorless pairing. Her mother must be away from the palace again, after some spat with him—although she never talked about their fights openly. *What was she doing following a fishmonger in the sea? What was she doing showing up in my dream? Who was the creature?* She liked to take her dreams apart, to unravel their messages, but this one was puzzling. *Maybe dreams don't mean a thing.* Her gaze shifted toward the moon, still high in its night sky. There would be hours still until morning. *But maybe,* she thought, forcing her eyes back shut, *they mean everything.*

TWO

As sure as the sun rises each day, Circe knew some dreams carry messages from Apollo, the god of light and music, and Morpheus, the god of sleep and slumber. Still, how remarkable that her mother, who had never approved of Odysseus because of his warrior past and cunning reputation, had shown up to test the amphibian. Was this a sign of approval?

Stepping outside her palatial home, built of cut stone and set on the hillside, she walked down the grand staircase to the nearby forest grove to find Odysseus. He was already up, gathering tools for his morning chores. Watching him prepare to return to the ship, the only ship that had survived his adventures, was like salt on her wound of abandonment. He had told her he planned to move the ropes onto the beach to inspect and repair them today.

Wild mountain wolves and lions prowled around them peacefully, for the enchantress had tamed and drugged them to be guardians of the island. Even Odysseus's swine men, who had feared them at first, appeared to ignore them. The mighty beasts had turned into friendly lambs, though their fierce growls surely sent shivers down the pigs' spines.

Circe covered her arms with a shawl, for the morning dew had not lifted yet, and sat on a bench. She was not an ordinary immortal but one that gods, including her parents, tracked closely; Apollo, Hermes, Poseidon, and others had meddled in her affairs. Their fascination with her stemmed from the way she had grown her powers through her patient and thorough exploration of Mother Nature, her taming of beasts, her unveiling the properties of herbs to heal and control. She was a powerful sorceress in the galaxy of immortals, one who could shape-shift and liked to engage with mortals.

Finishing her breakfast, Circe steepled her fingers and turned to Odysseus. "You won't believe it, but I think this fishmonger of yours, Glaucus, visited me in my sleep."

"Curious," Odysseus said, and asked her to recount her dream. Once she had finished, he told her it sounded like the fishmonger could be Glaucus.

"This dream is confusing. My Nana was exceptionally good at analyzing my dreams. I wish she were still alive and with me." Circe sighed. Her childhood caretaker, Nana, one of the few people she trusted, had nurtured her spirit of curiosity and adventure, and had been her solid companion in and out of her father's palace.

In the course of the conversation, divine Circe suspected that Odysseus had asked Apollo to help him extricate himself from her and her island, Aeaea. The dream Apollo had sent her was steering her attention to another man! Had her lover promised the god another sacrifice to coax him to intervene? Perhaps this suspicion would help her release him and his crew back to the sea.

"I wonder what Glaucus would have told me today about our return to Ithaca," Odysseus said, sounding worried. He stopped his search in a box filled with tools and begged her directly, "Circe, perhaps you have some advice for me? I need your help and wisdom to know how to best prepare for the journey." He had earned fame and praise for his leadership during ten years of guiding Greeks in the Trojan War. Since then, Circe had seen his love for glory and brave deeds shift to homesickness, a yearning to return and be with familial souls: Penelope, his wife; Telemachus, his son; and his aging father, Laertes.

She looked at him, scowling. "Odysseus, noble son of Laertes, was it Glaucus who told you how to prevent me from turning you into a swine?"

He chuckled. "You are still tracking him? No, no. It was Hermes. He met me on my way to your palace the day we arrived here and gave me the magic herb gods call moly, a black root with a milky white flower to use for my protection. That was my talisman."

"That's why you never changed shape, even though you drank my potion!" Her eyes glistened with her realization, once more, that the Olympians loved interfering in her life. To his question, she responded thoughtfully. "I know how much all of you have suffered at sea, and how many ills and cruel savages you had to overcome. You would get the best advice from Tiresias, but to find him you have another dangerous journey. Tiresias, the seer, is among the dead. It's worth it for you to descend into the shadows of Hades. You will meet ghosts that have haunting stories to share. Listen to them, but be sure to find him and hear him out."

He nodded, furrows of concentration on his face as he considered her words. "I have known no mortal who ever attempted to intrude into the realm of the dead."

She felt his burden, his weariness with such a destiny, and watched him turn away to leave her, drying with the back of his hand tears that trickled down his cheeks. Yet Circe believed that if anybody could, it would be noble Odysseus who could carry the weight of one more deadly challenge and succeed. She gazed after him as he started down the path to the beach, knowing he would spend the rest of his day contemplating Tiresias as he prepared his ropes.

Circe moved to the spinning house, her favorite morning room, to weave more magic on her upright, warp-weighted loom. Her tapestry was ethereal, painting worlds not known to men, with lively plants and animals that seemed to move about the land. It was a world of green and gold, white and silver threads only she could tame. She wove tirelessly, sending the shuttle across the tent of threads, using strings, silk threads, and ribbons with a steady hand. All along, she was thinking about Odysseus. Their days together would be over soon. Once he came back from Hades, he and his men would depart, leaving her alone. She sent the shuttle through the warp one last time and moved to drink some water. Then she combed her black hair and left the palace, making her way to the pigsty.

This time she was determined to learn more about Glaucus from Elpinikis. When the amphibian encountered Odysseus and his crew, what prophetic guidance had he offered? She approached the pigsty quietly and stopped behind some bushes.

The usual pessimism reigned among the men. One was grumbling, "Glaucus lied to us in Delos. We are never getting back home! Who says he helps fishermen and sailors like us? Another lie!"

Elpinikis shouted with alarm at the soldier, "Blasphemy! How many times must I remind you of the story about Glaucus and his powers? I don't want to hear your doubts. Remember how he told us about the properties of herbs, how important they are for the living? The herbs brought his fish back to life. We know Circe is famous for her potions; that's how she turned us into swine! And he knows rites too. Have some respect!"

Circe crept closer to the pigsty, spotted Elpinikis, and fixed her eyes on him. This time, she knew, he would not hesitate to share what he knew, because Odysseus had instructed him to speak freely and answer all her questions. An older soldier stopped rolling in the mud and asked him: "Is he really immortal? How do you know?" Some of the others snickered, but Circe's curiosity was piqued. She moved closer in, beyond the palm trees.

She watched Elpinikis's eyes dart around from the old soldier to her. "Circe, daughter of Helios," he called, "Glaucus spent months exploring the forest near his village, trying different herbs. In the end, he discovered the magic ones and used them to bring the fish he caught back to life. Then one day, fascinated by their properties, he ate some himself. It was a most amazing miracle; that was how he became immortal."

Circe guessed what happened next. "But gods exact a price for everything they grant. That must be when he shifted in form to a graceful amphibian creature, growing fins instead of arms and a fish tail instead of legs. Isn't that right, Elpinikis?"

"Yes. He knows how hard life is for fishmongers and sailors. That's why he offered us prophecies, to hearten us, to let us know we should trust in Odysseus. He told us we will sail again away from your spellbinding island. He would not lie. Would he, Circe?"

Now she stood among them. "No. Just as he said it. But Odysseus needs to get one more prophecy to help him on this journey. Then you will be on your way to Ithaca again." With that, she revealed the magic wand she always carried in her inside pocket and turned them back to men!

THREE

*T*hat afternoon, feverish preparations began near the palace to stage a celebration and an evening meal at the luscious grove. Circe had ordered that the symposium take place at the clearing, a flat expanse surrounded by palm trees and thick brush. Odysseus was to be treated as the king he was, and his men like the brave warriors they had proven to be in Troy.

Slave girls labored most of the day, decorating under Circe's watchful eye with fronds and flowers, and gathering all that was needed to serve food and wine and offer entertainment to the joyful assembly. They moved several couches to the clearing and set up tables in the middle to house the endless supply of food and drink. In the center they set a tall krater to store the wine and signal the upcoming celebration. It was decorated with figures of a Dionysian procession, ecstatic satyrs, and maenads playing their aulos, which were woodwinds much like oboes. They reserved a space with bench seats for the musicians who would entertain the party. Already the musicians were rehearsing melodic tunes they would perform at the gathering. In the palace kitchen, servants lit fires, cleaned fish, meat, and vegetables, and set cauldrons over coals to heat stock.

Another group of girls guided the men to the baths to prepare them for an evening of luxury. Several, deprived of male companionship on Circe's island, enjoyed their chance for quick, opportunistic pairings. They exchanged first glances, then embraces. Circe could hear the pleasures of lovemaking, moans escaping lips, betraying hungry entanglements in bathtubs filled with aromatic herbs. She counted them lucky, for her own desires had been well satisfied in the arms of Odysseus.

The men that the slave girls had bathed and dressed in white tunics slowly gathered in twos and threes at the grove. Tonight, Circe meant to make a memorable event, honoring their Trojan days and Odysseus's year on her island. Refreshed and cheery, they were led to their appointed couches where the girls of Aeaea helped them wash their hands. More greetings, jokes, and murmurs of appreciation filled the evening air.

The celebration was ordered in a way that all the men still remembered, despite the hardships of the war and their days in animal bodies that held them prisoners of Circe. Odysseus's men looked younger, as their wounds and scabs had healed, their beards were trimmed, their bodies were refreshed, and their spirits lifted.

Circe shared her couch with Odysseus as servants carried large platters with roasted fish garnished with fresh spices and a lemon-oil sauce. They passed trays with olives and cheese around as appetizers. Tables were covered with exotic fruit and greens prepared in the palace kitchen. Her palatial home had not put on a celebration like this in a century.

Later, satiated and content, the guests watched musicians arrive and start the entertainment as tables were cleared and preparations were made for the service of wine and more delicacies. The moon had risen over the horizon line when two musicians bent over their lyres and touched the strings, gently releasing haunting melodies from their Ithaca home. Elpinikis, now a handsome young man, started singing in a deep, rich, and clear voice. Homesick warriors, touched by familiar rhythms and textures of honey tunes, joined him, and the aulete sweetly played his pipes. They sang about life and death, the vanity of war, their love of women, wine, and home.

Under Melis's supervision, servers rushed to bring new offerings of cheese, fruit, nuts, raisins, and delicious figs that were passed around. When Odysseus stood up, silence fell over the grove. He spoke, his voice hoarse at first, and thanked Circe for the celebration. "Beautiful, mesmerizing Circe, we will never forget tonight. Your spirit of generosity to my men and your hospitality will remain legendary. May Zeus, Athena, and all the Olympians keep you strong and happy on your lovely island that gave us a chance to rest and gather our strength for the journey." His hands reached out toward her, then folded together in a motion of graceful thanks. She nodded, sexy and sublime, in her yellow silk tunic, a lace of spring flowers in her hair and her queenly smile lighting her face. She waved to her servers to fill all cylices with wine and bring around more food. A murmur of thankful toasts followed his words. They all raised their cylices to praise Circe, her tables, the musicians, and this celebration. She marveled that to the last man they held back their anger for the days they had been trapped in swine bodies.

The king of Ithaca continued, "I thank all gods, especially those that have helped and protected us all these years at war and at sea. Tonight, I offer a special thanks to Apollo, the son of Zeus, the god of light, music, and archery, for his gifts," and with that he tipped his cylix and poured libations to Apollo as his men cheered and praised the god.

Odysseus remained standing, appearing reluctant to return to the couch, as he would have done most any other time. He took a sip of wine and brought his finger to his lips to signal silence. The men leaned in to listen in a new hush. "Men of Ithaca, I have an announcement to make. Soon I will leave the island on a mission. I have one more journey to take, a journey to Hades."

Whispers of wonder and fear lifted from the grove, from his men and all the servants.

Odysseus continued, "I am going to seek the wisdom of the old seer, Tiresias, who resides among the dead. Even in Hades he is the greatest seer among men. Circe told me he will give me guidance for our safe return to Ithaca."

This time Circe stood up to toast the brave hero who, for the safety of his men and love of country, was willing to venture into Hades to secure guidance from the famous seer. The men, awed, took turns offering toasts, wishing him a safe trip and acknowledging his bravery for undertaking the dangerous descent. More food and music would carry the evening celebration until the small hours of the morning.

After the speechmaking, Circe sensed Odysseus was tired, preoccupied, and needed his rest before sailing his ship to the gates of Hades. She waited until the lyre finished releasing its melodious tune, then took his hands in hers and whispered, "Should we retreat and get you ready for your journey? I have a few more tips to give you." She had consulted her scrying mirror the week before and was ready to prepare him for his return trip.

They left the gathering without fuss, waving people to continue on celebrating. In the bedroom, Circe gave him more instructions. "Carry sacrificial lambs to Hades. When you cross the river Styx that separates the world of living from the dead, you must wait to meet and speak to those attracted by the blood. Listen to them, but wait for Tiresias. He will give you guidance."

Odysseus took her into his arms and kissed her, more gratefully than lovingly, his passion for her already satiated. They had shared a bed for several months. She turned, hugged him, and ran her fingers through his hair affectionately, wondering how many more nights they would be together.

"There is more to share tomorrow," she said. "Rest well, my dear."

In the night's slumber, trusty Morpheus delivered another dream to the enchantress sent from meddling Apollo. Alone, a fish-monger appeared, walking by the sea on a cloudy day, carrying a bucket with his catch and stuffing handfuls of moly into his mouth. Leaning in for a close-up, she saw he was attractive: kind hazel eyes, green-copper curly hair, thick neck, and robust muscles. His body was slowly growing scales that glowed, and she saw new fins and a tail sprout as he lost his arms, feet, and balance.

It had to be Glaucus. Fascinated by the magic of this human-turned-immortal who left the land to live in the deep and shallow waters, Circe tried to reach out and steady him. Even in a dream, her arms moved involuntarily toward the sky. But it was not to be. In a flash, the mighty Poseidon overtook the scene, gliding to the rescue. He wielded his trident once and reached the fishmonger, kindly lifting him in his wake to deep waters. She followed them as they rushed under the surface of the sea, and was relieved to see the god deposit startled Glaucus into the hands of his daughters, the Nereids, who soothed him and taught him about the sea. She saw his handsome face one more time, surprised and curious, still amazed, waking up to a miracle, and then he faded away.

Overwhelmed, she lost her sleep but stayed in her bed in the quiet of the night. Going over each scene, she recalled each detail, and then she knew that she had witnessed Glaucus's transformation! Her heart skipped a beat.

Was the bewitching queen of Aeaea getting bewitched?

FOUR

S leep came in cruel spurts to Odysseus that night. The road to Hades churns unpleasant dreams, even to the bravest. Wrestling with ghosts in his dreams, he returned outside the walls of Troy, amidst battles, blood, and life-and-death encounters with heroes and villains, till dawn. "Athena . . ." He summoned his protector goddess. "No, no . . ." Then he woke, dripping with sweat.

When the first light broke, he was still tossing and turning, exhausted. He woke up lying still and staring at the ceiling. Sun rays caught the chestnut highlights of Circe's hair; he stroked her lightly, arranging some strands, and as he was about to leave, he noticed her eyelids flutter. He shifted next to her warm body, hungry to taste her lips and trace her breasts. She sighed and took him into her arms. "Odysseus . . ."

Sometime later they rose for the first meal of the day and walked to the grove, which was abandoned by the merry men and tireless servants. As Circe braided her thick hair, he examined his sword, its sharp edge, wondering what he should take along on this new journey. "Who will show the way, Circe? What should I take with me?"

With nimble fingers, she continued braiding and set diamond-studded clips in her hair. "The north wind will guide your ship and your crew to Persephone's grove. Take some good men, walk across two rivers on foot, and once across, dig a deep

21

trench. There you will pour libations and sacrifice a ram and a black ewe to the gods, letting the blood pour into the trench. That is your invitation to the shadows of the dead."

Odysseus interrupted her, "Are we in danger? Should I set a guard?"

She continued evenly. "Stay alert and burn the sacrificial animals. Shadows will surge forward as you pray. Keep them away with your sword if they assemble; don't let them drink the blood." She held his eyes. "Summon Tiresias, the seer. He will drink the blood that gives him energy, and he will tell you about getting to Ithaca." Circe reached for her filmy robe and buckled a golden rhinestone belt around her waist. Then she tied a silk scarf on her head and moved down the stone steps of the staircase, with Odysseus following behind. "Odysseus," she said, "remember this time last year? When we gathered olives?"

It was soon after his arrival that she had taken him down a dusty path on the day before the picking was about to begin. "A wonderful grove, and as I recall, one you planted yourself, years ago," he responded.

A smile shaped her lips. He could see that she was proud of the grove, gratified to watch the trees she had seeded from olives on a flat expanse of the island flourish, nurtured by full sun. They were just getting to know each other. Odysseus had been eager to take part in the local harvest rituals and helped with the gathering. "A fine time," he acknowledged, flashing back to the procession of her crew carrying ladders, nets, and sticks that the goddess had led to the grove. She had stopped walking, turned, and repeated in her booming voice the traditional words of thanksgiving, as she did every year before the picking:

Praises be to Gracious Demeter, who leads us to this harvest,
Giving us another year of prosperity and peace.

To Odysseus she said, "You don't want to miss the season, dear. You and your men could give us a hand, join us in the labor and the celebrations before you start out on the challenging journey home—more rested, more refreshed, and better prepared for the labors of the seas."

He took her hand, and they walked side by side. He had come to realize that although not a particularly pious woman, she loved rituals and observed traditions, especially those she created for her people, and carried out tributes to gods. It was his turn to disappoint her. "My dear Circe, it was a fine time. I will remember it fondly, always. But my men are ready for the journey, and Penelope is waiting."

She looked sad for a moment, but then a spark of anger crossed her eyes. "Sometimes you remind me of Aeetes, especially when you refuse to hear me. My brother, the king of Colchis, is your equal: ungrateful and stubborn. He never shows up when he is needed."

Odysseus scratched his temple, puzzled. He knew she had not heard from Aeetes this past year, but he was eager to deliver his message. "It was quite a celebration you staged for my crew and soldiers last night, but a few may resent you for the year they spent in the pigsty, Circe. I don't want any harm to come to you while I am gone. Talk with Elpinikis, and I will too."

"I wish Aeetes would come to Aeaea while you are gone. He promised to stay here and keep me company, but it has been eons and I have not seen him on this island." Circe's laugh sounded bitter. "He would enjoy managing your men."

Odysseus knew the story. The two siblings had been close growing up, but when Aeetes turned sixteen, he rebelled against his father, refusing to join his soldiers who were preparing for battles. In a fury, Helios banished him from the palace, and that night the boy left Circe behind in his sudden departure for Colchis, by the Black Sea. Circe had pleaded, "Take me with you," for she was having troubles of her own with her very stern mother, but he slipped away, leaving her with a note she had carried to Aeaea. It was scribbled in a rush and delivered to her the next day: "Our time to go is now. I will visit you wherever you settle." He would know the place, being a sorcerer himself. It was her time to go too. A week later, Circe departed for Aeaea, letting only her Nana know her destination.

Now Odysseus leaned in reassuringly, held her hand, and told her, "Elpinikis is a capable man, my dear, and the men know him. Let him manage them, give them chores. They can prepare for our eventual departure; they can gather supplies and store them in the cave by the water's edge. I don't know how long I will be gone, but, Pluto willing, I will return soon, my sweet Circe."

He savored an appreciative look at the queen of the island. Their eyes met for an instant, but the selection of crewmen who would accompany him to the underworld already occupied his mind. Elpinikis, his loyal companion, would have some suggestions about who was suitable and would keep the rest busy.

Circe urged him, "Be stealthy and careful on this journey, brave son of Laertes. I will be here when you return to hear your stories and launch you on your way to Ithaca. Feel free to go about your day. I know you have a lot on your mind."

She spoke with a silvery voice, pushing down her true emotions, cherishing his attentiveness and the sweetness in his words, words of a mortal who cared for the safety of his goddess. She felt his affection. She had to reconcile herself to his pending departure and would miss him, but not for long.

All the while, Circe thought that his absence meant returning to long, quiet days working on her loom without interruption. She loved her weaving days, but in truth, Odysseus's presence and attentiveness had spoiled her this past year.

They had laughed, gossiped, and shared stories together. On long nights when he opened up, he spoke of Agamemnon, Menelaus, and Achilles, the Trojan War, his adventures at sea, and his younger years in Ithaca. She liked it better when he spoke about "going on hunting trips with Argos, my dog and best companion." A smart, brave, and lustrous royal himself, he was a worthy companion. Yes, she would miss him, yet she cared enough to let him go and see him safely back to Ithaca.

On her way to the grove, she turned her thoughts to last night's dream and the miraculous transformation of Glaucus. She relived the moments of his metamorphosis and shivered with excitement, overpowered by the intoxicating experience. His inexplicable charm had captured her even though she had not yet seen him in the flesh. Was his hair curly and abundantly thrown about his shoulders? Were his eyebrows large and thick above his hazel eyes, or was the dream deceiving? How was it living in the sea in the company of the Nereids? Her curiosity was mixed with fascination. It wouldn't be hard to pay the island of Delos a visit while Odysseus was away; it was an opportune time. She clapped her hands, and servant girls appeared at once to clear the area around her and take her order. All she wanted for breakfast was some freshly picked lotus fruit.

The next morning, Odysseus and his crew met on the ship. They loaded the ram and the ewe they had taken from Circe's herd and prepared to set sail. He sometimes talked to himself, not only out of habit but because that was how he had trained his crew to know what he wanted.

"Circe has sent us a brisk wind to fill our sails." Hearing his words, a whoosh of zephyrs picked up their speed and Odysseus pointed to the sails. "Look, we are moving fast. Keep them full, men, all the time. We will land in Persephone's grove in a day or two."

25

The loyal sailors who accompanied Odysseus, although anguished with the thought of Hades, felt the weight of yet another adventure into the unknown. Catching the wind, they sang out, as they eased the sheets to breathe: "Thank you . . . thank you, loyal Circe," grateful for her help and their leader's ties to her. They trusted the winds guided them safely and that they were on course to the mists and clouds of the House of Death.

"Our hopes and fortunes are sealed with yours, Odysseus. We depend on you and the goodwill of the mighty gods," vowed the eldest one.

"We will sacrifice the animals as soon as we reach the Gates of Hades," said Odysseus. "Keep a tight rein on them. Their blood will appease the Olympians and let us reach the seer, Tiresias."

With that, the crew drew lots, setting their day and night watches for the journey.

FIVE

T he palace, noisy though it was, felt empty in the absence of Odysseus, and the thought that these sailors were heading to the underworld troubled Circe. That first day she worked on her loom, mechanically sending the shuttle back and forth until, inspired, she took some white, gray, and black skeins of thread from her pile and started weaving the shape of a pair of dolphins, floating in a dreamy skyline like birds in flight. She hoped they found Odysseus. They would be congenial, protective companions for the ship. The rhythm of her loom was soothing. The day rolled on uneventfully as the palace filled with Odysseus's crew in its halls.

Restless that evening, she stayed up late talking with handsome Elpinikis, the man Odysseus had put in charge of the crew he had left behind. She heard him approaching gingerly, saw him keeping a close eye on a pair of wolves loitering nearby, and waved him to come closer. "They won't hurt you," she promised. He was short, his skin olive, his tunic freshly laundered. She had already noticed he was built of muscle and carried a certain authority over the men. They settled on the porch; the breeze was gentle.

Elpinikis was grateful for her hospitality. "At your service, Circe," he said respectfully in his deep, pleasing voice.

"Odysseus and the ship are on course," she said, and he knew she meant to comfort him. He nodded, although worry still lingered in his mind. Then she added, "While you are in charge of the men here, make sure they know my bedroom and spinning house are off-limits."

He shifted, eager to please her. "They will know not to bother you." He had already realized that only a few trusted servants who knew and managed her needs unobtrusively had direct access to her, and he was pleased that she had called on him today.

"Let me know if you have any problems here."

She seemed friendly, and he knew to follow her orders. "Of course." Still, the responsibility weighed on him. One never knew what trouble sailors could get into. "How long before Odysseus returns?" he ventured.

"It won't be long," she assured him.

He looked at her, sensing that she was reassuring herself at the same time, for this was a critical moment.

"Odysseus is close to the entrance to Hades. He is well prepared for the adventure. I did all I could to help." Then she moved a step closer. "This Glaucus. What led you to him?"

"We saw people seeking him out in Delos. They told us he had received a god-given blessing and they were asking him what their futures held. He has the gift of prophecy. We needed to have safe passage to Ithaca, and he was willing to help us."

"How did he help you?"

"He taught us how to appease the gods, initiating us into the cult of Poseidon, who has a temple on Delos, the silver island. He taught us the rites and prophesied that our ship would land on your island. He predicted that here we would rest and gather provisions to continue on our journey home."

Circe had already known Glaucus's name meant "glimmer of the sea." She surmised the name was a true attribution to his nature and trusted he had a good reputation. Odd that she had never heard of him before.

Elpinikis's descriptions stayed with her that night. Not only did Glaucus know about herbs, but he was immortal and had the gift of prophecy; he also knew about her island. Intrigued, Circe felt a strong desire to meet him, drawn to the mystery of his transformation as she fell into a deep sleep.

The next day, the enchantress ordered her morning meal in her room. She needed to put her thoughts in order. Driven by her loneliness, she considered all the information about Glaucus in a positive light. There were a lot of coincidences. He was showing up in her dreams just as Odysseus and his men were about to depart. Were these dreams suggestions for the future?

She took a bite of her omelet and looked out of the window. "Nana, what do you think? Should I? Would you encourage me to explore the possibilities?" She did not expect an answer.

Her Nana had been a priestess who had served in Apollo's temple. Circe's mother chose her to look after her daughter because of her reputation as an educator for the temple community. She was loving and dedicated to Circe, guiding her in how to make decisions, what to learn, and what to avoid. Circe remembered the afternoon she had left her father's home without letting anyone know. "Mother's dog was chasing a squirrel, and I followed them," she had said unapologetically. The nine-year-old adventurer was about to get a sound scolding, and Nana interceded when an angry Perse appeared ready to hit Circe. But Nana, with her eyes on the floor, stepped in front of young Circe and took the blame for losing track of her. She had nearly lost her job, but never blamed the child.

Like a member of the family, Nana would saunter with Circe to Helios's throne room and coax him to take her for rides on his gilded chariot: "Show her how you bring the light to the world, O Helios!"—a treat that was thrilling for Circe. Nana encouraged the child's risk-taking and often accompanied her in her explorations. She had taught her to love life, nature, and all creatures.

Even with no answer from Nana, it was obvious: there was no better time to meet this kind god and get to know him. Would they get along? Well, who knew, though from a place of knowing more, she figured she could make a better decision about pursuing him. Was the "prize" worth the price of making room for another partner? Finding a compatible companion who was immortal had definite appeal, but she was way ahead of herself.

While the kitchen girls were busy feeding the men dinner, she ventured out to greet her wild companions, the mountain wolves and lions. They hovered, curious, close to the palace, circling around her, ready to accompany her anywhere. She took the path up the hill that led to her small temple where she honored and sacrificed to the Olympians. It seemed prudent to keep them on her side.

Carrying wine and honey, she planned to offer a libation to the master of the seas. When she arrived and approached the altar, she ceremoniously poured the mix from a silver bowl. With her arms uplifted, she beseeched Poseidon for guides that would safely take her to Glaucus's abode. Then she drank the remaining mix and returned to her palace feeling that the god would respond.

Poseidon had heard her. That night, he appeared in her dream in all his majesty, stirring the waters with his trident, then he pointed into the distance. Three gentle dolphins were swimming swiftly toward the shore, and Circe understood that they were to carry her to the island of Delos.

The next morning, she returned to the rocky promontory and checked the horizon line for dolphins. It was a chilly walk, as the wind and the rain pounded the island hard. It was not to be that day. Disappointed and impatient, she returned to her palace.

Elpinikis was waiting for her at the great hall. He had turned out to be a likable man, polite, with short black hair and a trim beard. His voice, commanding, carried and got the attention and obedience of the crew. He carried a walking stick wherever he went, one he had carved himself of cherrywood he had retrieved in Aeaea. Circe had watched him work on it and admired his patience and skill; it was neat and even, with a continuous meander running along its sturdy length.

As she approached him, he said to her, "I need to identify supplies for the ship that will feed the crew for days at sea. Your servants suggested dried fruit like figs, raisins, olives, and preserved fish and meats. Whom shall I coordinate with in the kitchen?"

Circe appointed her faithful Melis, the oldest among her servants, to assist Elpinikis. There were medicinal herbs to take along to treat common ailments like colds and migraines, skin and surface wounds. She told him to remind Melis to give him the supply she would prepare for them herself. Then she informed him she would be gone for a few days but did not disclose where she would be.

That afternoon, she returned to the palace and went directly to her loom, suddenly anxious that all her recent dreams might be misleading; maybe they were more about her desires than predictions for the future.

On the third day, she returned to the promontory to wait for the sun to rise. It was a glorious morning. The waters were calm and there was no breeze. Once more she searched the horizon, and this time she spotted dolphins. There were three, jumping, taking high leaps and turns, approaching the island, their compass set to the cape. She waved and moved closer to meet them, excited like a sixteen-year-old about to be a seafaring queen, exuberant, soon to travel to meet a new suitor.

SIX

*T*wo of the dolphins were spinners, leaping and sliding, playing young, fancy-free games. The third was large and calmer, and all three moved together in perfect harmony. Circe trusted their sense of direction and intelligence, grateful that they would play a part in her new adventure. After all, they were progenitors to humans, known pirates of the seas, familiar with the immense blue vistas of the Mediterranean, the most fascinating and dangerous maritime relatives of the human species. The word was that in days bygone, Dionysus, the god of wine and theater, facing a band of pirates who were about to kidnap him, transformed these saltwater outlaws into the first dolphins. Graceful and playful, they caught Poseidon's attention. He chose them to be his special messengers and often sent them on as his emissaries.

She saw them smile and encourage her to swim out to where they could pick her up and embark on their distant mission. Circe walked in, feeling the chill of the sea, then plunged in boldly. When she reached them, she climbed onto the largest one, who had sunk under the water's surface to lift her up and waited for her to settle close to his flipper. She clung on as the other two greeted her with trills and grunts, keeping her in their midst. They moved at a good clip, synchronized and gliding along the surface.

By noon, they had slowed down to rest, floating on calm waters. Circe jumped into the deep water and swam alongside them. It was an exhilarating journey with playful companions, but by sunset she was cold and tired. Surrounded by the dark night sky, she remembered the time Odysseus pointed to the stars, the Pleiades and Orion that marked seafaring routes for all travelers, and raised her eyes to the sky. In the plethora of steady, blinking, and fading dots, she recognized the constellations. Did the dolphins study and track them? she wondered. Then she held on to her companion and shut her eyes.

That night, in her dream, Glaucus came again, this time mingling in the merry company of Nereids, the sea nymphs, holding a lively conversation that ended up in laughter. Although she could not make out their words, Circe admired the gathering, wishing she could join them. A garden of starfish, sea anemones, and tall kelp surrounded them, and they rested on seats made of coral and shimmering sands that floated in the turquoise waters. Was this an invitation?

It was daylight when she woke up, in time to view the port of Delos in the distance. Ships from every corner of the Mediterranean crowded the bay. In the early morning hours, fishermen worked on their nets, emptying last night's catch into containers, getting ready for market. On the hill, above the market, Circe could see the monumental gateway to the temples, the Propylaea, and beyond it all the sanctuaries that silver Delos was known for.

The first order of her day would be to visit the temple dedicated to the twelve gods to offer libations to Poseidon, a god popular on this seafaring island. Close to it was the famous Delian temple of Apollo. Circe suspected it was he who had sent her Morpheus to deliver dreams about Glaucus. Her visit to Delos might have been all his plotting, and she admittedly did rather enjoy it. Perhaps she would have to stop by and honor him as well.

The dolphins approached the landing and waited until she safely stepped onto the deck. Then, with a flourish and a whistle, they were off to run new errands for Poseidon. She rested, dried in the scorching sun and looked around her, examining the town to get her bearings. There were few people on the shore. She approached a craggy old fishmonger repairing his nets. "Hello, stranger. I do not know my way around Delos. I just arrived and want to thank Poseidon. Where do I find sacrificial animals for the gods?"

The old man looked up from his nets, his neck taut. Taking in her tall form and her glow, he gulped, dropped his thread, and bowed to Circe. By the brightening of his eyes, she could see that he had heard of her—the famous sorceress who lived on Aeaea. He straightened his curved shoulders, raised his arm, and pointed to the hill. "That is the way to the temples, my goddess. Beyond the Propylaea, you will find sellers with an abundance of offerings to purchase. But why would you need to get goods when you are a glorious goddess, one among them?"

"I have come to pay my respects this morning. I am not one of the Olympians, my good man. I am the daughter of Helios, exiled from his palace; I am the one who lives among wild beasts on my island, Aeaea." She paused and smiled, amused by his curiosity, and returned an ambiguous look. "It may not be a gift to be an immortal. I want to live like a mortal during my stay in Delos, just like Glaucus used to be before he turned up here. By the way, where will I find him?"

She could see that he did not fear her, old and wise as he was, and that he knew she had no reason to target him; he simply answered that she should travel to the south side of the island. "It is where occasionally people go swimming, where young men go searching for their girls; there you will find Glaucus." Then in a gossipy whisper he added, "There are many beauties on this island; some have not committed their hearts to anyone yet and young men seek them out."

Circe thanked him and walked to the hillside to spend the day on the parched landscape, exploring sanctuaries and mingling among the devout and the temple servants. Soon she was crossing the Propylaea and saw a busy lineup of vendors offering souvenirs, pottery, and all manner of trinkets and sacrificial animals for the gods. She scanned the goods available and settled on a pair of restless goats, spirited and whimsical, befitting the chancy nature of her adventure.

Approaching the tallest priest of three, she told him to take one goat and dedicate her offering to Poseidon. Nodding, he took the animal to the altar in front of the temple, as her voice rose: "In the light of day and under the stars of night, your swift messengers carried me safely to the sacred isle. Thank you, Poseidon, master of the seas, leader of the nymphs, for my companions at sea and all your gifts." Watching the knife plunge into the goat's neck, she saw its feet kick and the blood flow into a silver bowl. "I have come to find what joy may await me here."

When the sacrifice was over, she motioned to the temple servants to take the spoils and share the feast among themselves. Then she moved on. She could not have missed the Delian temple of Apollo, for it was the largest on the site. A rich temple, surrounded by simple, elegant Doric columns, it was the depository of many precious offerings the pious had brought to the god's birthplace over the centuries. The bystanders sensed her special place and made room for her as she approached the priests. She handed them her offering, and they carried it to the altar. This time she willed the goat to be still in the priest's hands. "To you who rises and brings the sun to us each day, Apollo," she began, as the bloodletting sacrifice progressed, "I bring you an offering to thank you for light, music, and the dreams you send to gods and mortals alike."

She stood by to watch the smoke rise and saw that Apollo had accepted her offering. Pleased, she walked on and toured the sites. The path led her to the proud lions of Delos that lined the terrace, still and majestic. The marketplace was busy with men and women, mostly local. People made room for her to pass by, for she stood out by her height and carriage. She walked past the empty theater and did not stop to rest until she found a luxurious villa known as the House of the Dolphins, which she found open to visitors. She walked up a few steps, entered the central room, and leaned against the wall to take in the sight. A row of columns surrounded the interior atrium, and there was the famous mosaic. The workmanship of the floor exceeded her expectations in artistry and composition. Dolphins were leaping in the air; some were submerged in a gentle circle. She visualized them dancing and flipping off the floor as if they were alive. It was a marvelous site, an enchanted place. She lingered in the shade, staying away from the sun for a while, and splashed water on her face from the fountain in the center of the courtyard.

Circe stayed in the area all day, enjoying the atmosphere and meeting people from near and far who shared stories about what brought them to the island. The best part was running into an older man at the House of Dolphins who had sought the seer to ask for his help. He was friendly and chatty, a tall man, tan and weathered from the sea and the Greek sun. She had overheard him admiring the pairs of dolphins in the floor mosaic of the house, especially those with winged riders, and he thought Glaucus should be depicted with wings in Delos homes. The island claimed him. "He is our local, approachable, miracle god," said the older man. "He helped me when I lost my brother."

Circe followed him outside. "I overheard you talking about Glaucus. Is he a local deity?"

"He is a kind god. He helped me find my brother when he was lost in the forest," he replied, turning to speak to her, pleased with her attention.

"You were lucky to get help," she said, leaning against a column. She used her charming smile to invite conversation.

The man was eager to share his story. "You must be new here; everyone knows Glaucus. He has helped others too."

"When did you ask for Glaucus's help?"

"My brother was on a hunting trip but did not return home. We searched for him for two days. That is when I asked Glaucus for help. My wounded brother was struggling between life and death when we found him. Glaucus healed his wounds with herbs from the sea."

"Quite a story." She couldn't help but be impressed. "Where did you find Glaucus to get his help?"

"By his rock, at the beach," he answered.

"My good man, would you show me where that rock is?"

"I have plenty of time on my hands today," he said, examining her carefully. He smiled. "You are from out of town?"

"Aeaea is my island, beyond the horizon line," she answered vaguely.

"Do you need his help?"

"No, just curious to meet him." She looked away.

They walked side by side away from the sanctuary crowds. His name was Leo. He was an easygoing, hospitable man willing to go out of his way. Circe never shared her name, remaining charming and mysterious.

"Your island is so beautiful," she went on, as sand replaced the dust in her sandals.

When they reached the shore, he led the way. Her eyes followed the direction he was pointing to and saw the huge rock rooted in the bottom of the sea. It was an easy marker to find for those seeking advice.

Circe learned Glaucus came to the rock every day and swam around the bay. He had helped the worried man until his brother recovered. "I went to him in despair, fearing my brother lost. He guided me through the forest, giving me exact directions. He helped dispel my fear and deadness of action, and once we found him, he taught me how to use his algae medicine to heal my brother's wounds."

A slow smile formed on her lips as she listened to his story. Touched by Glaucus's caring ministrations, Circe was determined to get to know him better. She decided to stay on Delos until Odysseus returned from his mission in Hades.

The moon was coming out when they arrived at the southwestern beach. The smoky rock stood tall and massive; it was a spectacle she could not have imagined. The dark, rippling water reflected pale rays, and calmly and endlessly licked the rock's sturdy base. Parting, Leo wished her a pleasant stay in Delos and bade her goodnight, leaving her to look for a place to settle for the night.

SEVEN

That night she rested under the pine trees by the shore, filled with anticipation. Circe did not feel alone as she walked along the shore, listening to the rustle of the waves, soothed by the flickering stars of the night sky. She had found the beach and the barren rock where Glaucus usually turned up. She had always been attracted to unraveling mysteries, the unknown. The thought of his shape-shifting enchanted her, and his willingness to help humans was endearing. She told herself: *This urge to get to know him may be just folly. Who really knows another through and through?* She was here to be carried along the mystifying course her Fates had laid out.

Goddess to god, she had dreamed and pined for his attention, even a union, and knowing nothing lasts forever, she secretly hoped for a long affair. He must be generous, because people knew him to respond with prophecies to questions and grant their requests. The man she had met gave her proof he had benefited from Glaucus's help. All she could see in him was kindness, loyalty to his mission, and the gift of prophecy. She was nursing an infatuation, and the night was beguiling and endless.

With her arms raised toward the east, she greeted the new day gratefully. "Praise Poseidon, for bringing me safely ashore . . . May this day bring more delights . . ." But she paused when she noticed a young woman at the beach getting ready to swim.

When the girl saw Circe, she stopped. Apparently sensing that this was not an ordinary woman, she paid her tribute. "Welcome to Delos, my goddess, an island where we adore and respect our gods. My name is Skylla."

"Skylla, an unusual name," Circe commented, for in Greek the word means "female dog." "I love the company of four-legged creatures."

"You would like my furry friend. Her name is Melina. She waits for me at home. Her eyes are dazzling; her black fur is soft." She was young, a luscious, bosomy woman, tall and limber.

Circe said, "Your pious island raises beautiful women. Are you here to swim?"

"If I would not disturb you." The girl took a few steps backward away from the water.

"Come back later. I am about to swim myself." Then Circe walked down to the shallow water. Dipping her toes in, she lingered to get over the shivers and then dove into the bay. She swam out, much beyond where she could touch the sandy bottom, and dog-paddled for a while. Then she floated on her back, feeling the sun warm her through, blinding her vision. Living by water was a blessing and this was a welcome, loving embrace. To cool down she took a dive, aiming for the bottom. An octopus sped away and a school of tiny smelt passed by. She had not been swimming in recent years and was overcome with how much life thrived in Poseidon's realm. Scanning around, she noticed something large coming from below. She focused on it and discerned an unusual creature, part man, part fish. It was him!

Glaucus had been traveling through the turbulent seas of the Aegean, from a neighborhood close to the shorelines of Delos, to reach the rendezvous beach. It was the usual time he approached the shore to court Skylla, the young woman with whom he was in love. His body shimmered in the turquoise waters, and he smiled warmly when he saw Circe. The moment she met him, she breathed him in, claiming his soul, hoping for his acceptance. When she looked at him, a liquid sweetness poured into her heart. She found honey in his eyes.

Glaucus was pleased to see her. Apollo had told him that one day he would meet her and wanted this to be a special welcome for the goddess he considered a peer.

Without words, they danced as if the music of sirens harmonized their movements. He graciously held her by her waist, guiding her steps; they quietly moved into thalassic depths, in the shimmering blue waters. Far behind him he had left a company of Nereids preening and chatting. Glaucus had found a hospitable home with them, and they had taught him the art of prophecy.

Although he loved Circe's gracefulness and her receptive response to his dancing leads, his mind was elsewhere. He had noticed that Skylla, a youth more beautiful than many goddesses, was not swimming as she always did but had settled under the shady pines on the beach. Was there something wrong that kept her on land?

He stopped dancing and escorted the goddess toward the rock. When he spoke, he felt awkward delivering his message. "Dear Circe, I am expecting a supplicant the temples are sending for a confidential exchange. Dancing with you was lovely. Please come back so that we may have a longer visit."

With shock, she realized she was being dismissed. The dancing—he tall and majestic—had convinced her she had to be with him. As they emerged from the sea, she had admired his copper-green hair and robust built, and felt that she would follow him willingly . . . but he was sending her away! How could this be?

She struggled for poise. After all, she had just shown up unannounced and did not want to disrupt the precious moments they had shared by being disagreeable. Landing a quick peck on his cheek, she questioned, "Tomorrow then?" He nodded. Facing the open sea, she swam toward the port. When she reached the harbor, she climbed up to the promenade and sat in the blazing sun to dry. Yesterday's old fishmonger was still mending his nets by the landing. When she approached him, he stopped his work and searched her eyes. "Did you find all you were looking for, O Circe?"

"Your guidance was excellent. I love your island. I may never leave Delos!" she said exuberantly.

"The Delian nets are strong and catch a lot of fish," he said, winking, as if he knew she had been caught.

"Tell me, who is Skylla?"

"She is our local beauty. Many young men seek her, Circe, but she is not as beautiful as you."

She laughed easily, her vanity satisfied, and started for the Propylaea, to spend another afternoon among the pious.

EIGHT

The hours of daylight dwindled. Leaving the noise and crowds of the temples, Circe returned to the familiar beach where she had spent the night before. She settled under the Delian pines and let the crackle of fragrant needles, the whispers of the evening breeze, and the lapping of the waves sing her lullabies. Her thoughts returned to Glaucus, legendary for saving sailors from rough seas. He had been so perfect, welcoming her with a thrilling, unexpected dance. Shivers of excitement ran down her spine as she recalled the moments they had moved together. It had been a silent dance that spoke of his grace and beauty. She had to find out more about him. With that thought, she shut her eyes and fell into a peaceful sleep.

In the morning, two chatty young lads awakened her. She thought they came to seek Glaucus's advice. There was life on this beach worth observing. She might learn more about this god by hovering. The lazy winds caressed the filmy veils that Circe wore as she roamed near the once-molten rock used as a place for consultation with Glaucus.

The lads dropped their conversation to a whisper when they saw Skylla arrive for her morning swim. "I wonder if she will talk to us," said the young man with a golden ring and a walking stick.

His handsome companion, tilting his head, answered confidentially, "There are too many of you lining up to claim her.

Just remember what I told you, she cannot resist presents. I wish you good luck, my friend."

Skylla glanced at the boys, turned to the water, and got ready for her swim. Circe, who recognized her from the day before, shape-shifted into a plain brown sandpiper, nervously bobbing its tail, and hopped near her, taking time to circle around to examine her. The woman was a beauty and had age on her side. Her long, flyaway chestnut hair floated around her face, and she pushed it to the side to uncover a pair of almond-shaped brown eyes. Her figure, trim and lanky, reminded the enchantress of Aphrodite. Slender and agile, she dropped her clothes and sandals on the sand and moved straight into the sea. The buoyant waters carried her limber body as she moved on the surface, floating at first and then swimming into deep waters.

Circe envied the lads' youth, and their plotting prattle entertained her. The boys were adolescents, stubble shadowing their upper lips. Hot hormones rushed through their bodies, lighting fires for Skylla, who was in her prime. The sorceress, who had made herself so tiny, nearly invisible, approached them to listen.

The lad with the black curly hair and the ring said, "I hope she likes gold," and then, excited, he piped up again: "Let's hide her clothes. She will have to talk to us, ask for help."

"She might get angry, or she might not. I think it's worth a try," his friend answered, snickering.

They both approached the water. "Look! She swims like a dolphin!" the boy with the ring declared, and bent down to pick up her clothes.

"I hope she doesn't disappoint you," his companion answered. They moved away to hide her white tunic, belt, hat, and leather sandals behind some bushes, and they crouched down to hide and wait.

When Skylla returned to shore, she lay down on some soft hay over the sand to dry in the sun's warmth. She checked around as if to make sure she had the beach to herself, but that did not last. Circe returned to her human form and drew near her, wanting to make conversation. It was her shadow that alerted Skylla to her presence. "Did you come to the beach to seek Glaucus's advice?" Circe asked.

Skylla sat up abruptly, clearly alarmed. She looked at Circe, covered her breasts, and scanned the shore for her clothes.

"We are not alone," Circe continued. "A pair of admirers are hiding just beyond the bushes. They took your clothes."

Skylla looked in the direction the goddess was pointing and shouted, upset, "Bring me my clothes!" She remained crouched down, shielding her bare body. In an instant, Circe, with a high wave of her wand, dressed her up in a loose golden tunic that accented her colors. The young woman, her eyes wide open, felt the fine silk with her fingertips, tossed her hair in the breeze, and thanked Circe with a quick bow.

As the boys approached them, Skylla answered her earlier question, "People come to seek Glaucus's advice. I am not one of them. I have been coming to this beach since I was a child."

The goddess contemplated the beach, listening to the lapping water. "It is peaceful here," she said, and urged the boys, "Come closer. Give her clothes back." Then she spoke to Skylla in a conciliatory tone, "The boys mean no harm. They want to flirt with you."

"Who are you, my goddess? You must be one of the Olympians."

"I am Circe, from Aeaea."

The boys, who had witnessed the conversation, were awed. They rushed to give Skylla her clothes back. "It was just a joke," the blond, handsome boy said, handing her the bundle shyly.

"I have seen you before," answered Skylla, returning a smile as she put on her sandals.

"Yes, at the agora, just yesterday," he answered eagerly.

"Talk to her in the village," Circe scolded him. "Do not disturb her morning swim."

The lads looked heartened, ready for a conversation. "We meant no harm."

Skylla put on her hat and followed Circe to the shade of the pine trees. Ignored, the boys withdrew, taking the path that led to the village, occasionally looking back, whispering to each other.

As the women were about to settle into a conversation, they heard a loud swish coming from the smoky rock. It startled Circe. The waters swirled around and broke, crashing loudly, and Skylla said, "He has arrived."

NINE

C irce moved closer to the rock to welcome his arrival. *He loves a grand entrance,* she thought. But she noticed Skylla had stayed behind, put her sandals on and tied her belt over her shimmering tunic. *Hmmm,* thought Circe. *She has seen him arrive a thousand times already and is no longer impressed by the commotion.*

He surfaced, kelp adorned, green-copper hair first, and surveyed the beach, his hazel eyes resting on Skylla. His face relaxed. Then he noticed Circe, his surprise evident, and greeted her warmly. He settled in the shallow waters, leaning on the tall rock, only his trunk visible above water. "Welcome to Delos, enchanted Circe. I see you have met Skylla."

"She is a lovely young lady. Yes, we met," she said, wondering if she was trespassing.

Circe realized then that Skylla was hurrying to follow the boys. Halfway to the path, the girl called out. "Circe, have a pleasant stay on our island. I have to leave you. Father is waiting. Again, thank you for your help and the lovely tunic."

"What help?" Glaucus called to the lass, but she did not turn back.

Circe quickly told him about the conspiring boys, Skylla's embarrassment, and the tunic she had conjured up to cover her youthful body. She noticed that Glaucus frowned and kept looking in the path's direction.

"Is everything all right?" Circe asked him.

"Yes, fine, fine . . . I wondered what her hurry was. But tell me, have you been touring Delos?"

Bending the truth a little, she answered, "A long time ago, I promised to come to Delos and offer a sacrifice to a god I owe a lot to. These past two days, I visited the sanctuaries beyond the Propylaea and admired the marble temples. Keeping my promise, I offered a sacrifice to Apollo, the god of music and light."

"It's great to have an Olympian protect you, Circe. Poseidon has been good to me. I have found a home in his kingdom. Tell me, what brings you here?"

"I heard about you from Odysseus and his men, who have been living on my island this past year. You and I share a lot of expertise in the ancient arts, Glaucus. We even share a significant interest in nature. At birth you were a mortal, a fishmonger; I was one of the many ordinary nymphs, a bride of the sea. I rose only after studying the dark arts, foraging for herbs, mastering the use of cauldrons, and gaining a powerful wand. So I wanted to meet you."

He seemed pleased that the famous sorceress recognized his knowledge. "On herbs of the land I am a beginner, compared to you, Circe, but I have been searching and learning more about properties of life under the sea since the gods willed me to live in its unfathomable world." But Circe could see into his heart and knew the truth was he missed roaming the forests to find herbs and his simple life as a fishmonger, although the sea had been fascinating to explore.

She watched his body glisten in the shallow waters, and though she hadn't thought about collaborating before, she said excitedly, "I hope you will share some of this knowledge with me."

"I recently discovered a new variety of algae that has healing properties," Glaucus said. "I've been eager to share, but no one has been as interested as you are in the medicinal properties of sea plants."

She plied him with a thousand questions. He explained where he located them, the water and sunlight conditions, their distinct characteristics. When she inquired about how he knew the plants had healing qualities, he told her he had used them to heal an infection an island priest suffered from.

"But now a new area of research has engaged my curiosity: Would my algae work as well dried up, as a powder, after being stored?"

She, too, was a curious researcher at heart. Intrigued about adding this remedy to her collection, Circe spoke about partner herbs that might strengthen its effect on humans and animals. They discussed other applications, and Glaucus agreed to bring her some samples to examine and perhaps experiment with.

Two hours had slipped by, and they had been deep in conversation when Circe asked him if they ever used potions during underwater celebrations. He laughed and confessed, "Sometimes—I cannot deny it, but we avoid potent stimulants. We use herbs to treat anxieties."

"It's a good way, in the hands of people who know how to use mushrooms and herbs," she said. Glaucus named a couple of sea plants he collected for these rituals; they were new to her, and she took note. Then she looked at him, and with a seductive smile she brought up the previous day's meeting. "By the way, you are a superb dancer, Glaucus. So relaxed! I would dance with you again."

He smiled. "The sea is a marvelous teacher; it has taught me to dance. And you were a wonderful partner. A unique way to meet you, Circe. I am also glad you met Skylla. I am fond of her. She swims like a creature of the sea."

"She has been here on both mornings." Circe focused on him with watchful eyes.

"Yes, she loves the sea. When she comes, young, immature boys always trail her. I wish they would leave her alone," he grumbled.

"But they are her age. It's her time," said Circe. "It's wonderful to see. She is such a lovely young woman."

"That she is! I do like her, but she recently seems to avoid me," he said, looking away.

Is he after the girl? "Are you sure?"

Glaucus flaunted his shiny tail, swishing it above water, and turned away, "Look, it's time I move on. I will look for the algae we talked about and will meet you here tomorrow, if that fits with your day."

"Same time tomorrow, then," said Circe.

He dove into the sea with impressive force, raising his tail in the air, and then sank under the water.

He loves grand exits too, she thought. She had found a way to connect, and she still loved his dashing form and sharp mind.

TEN

The old fishmonger looked up, showing no surprise to see Circe back at the promenade. He had gathered his nets and moved them onto his fishing boat. He spent most of his days on the small skiff, which provided for his livelihood. She found him resting on the thwart, sorting his mending needles and untangling the skeins of thread. When she arrived, he stopped organizing his tools, took off his fishmonger's hat, and greeted her with a nod. "Welcome, Circe. How can I be of service today?"

She had noticed the special eye painted on the side of the hull, the green iris and black pupil, the sign of a pious man who trusted in the guidance of gods. She smiled her "good morning" and his face beamed. She knew he was grateful for the honor she paid him as she had singled him out from all the other fishermen. People had noticed his divine visitor and had bought all of his catch this morning. She inquired kindly. "What is your name, my good man?"

"Aristos, my goddess," he said, and respectfully bowed his head.

A suitable name, she thought. Someone so dutiful should be called "the best." "And how long have you lived in Delos?"

"I was born here."

Ah, well, he must be special. Not surprising, then, that her intuition had led her to him from the first day; he had been responsive and a good source of information.

"Whose son are you, Ariste?"

"My father is Apollonius, no longer in life, a shadow in Hades, and my mother is Erato; her name means 'divine flower.' Mother is the daughter of Doris, the mother of Nereids. She abandoned the sea for the love of Apollonius and returned to it after his death. My brother is a temple priest of Poseidon."

Circe realized this brother had to be one of the three priests—the one with a graying beard—who had received her when she offered her sacrifice. She settled on the hard, slippery bulkhead steps next to his boat to ply him with more questions.

"Are you married with children?"

"The sea is an alluring mistress. She leaves no room for family."

"One among many," she answered cryptically. It was time to steer the conversation to her quest. She planned to forage for native herbs.

"Where would I find a verdant hillside thick with trees and plants and interesting herbs, Ariste?" she inquired. He suggested exploring the west side of the island, but the neighboring island of Mykonos was greener. When he fell quiet, she went on, "Tell me more about Skylla, her family and friends?"

"You have met her, then. She is the daughter of my young aunt who passed away a long time ago, and comes from a line of sailors, many still at sea most of the year. She used to live near the beach with the rock until she lost her brother to waves that crashed his boat. They found him washed ashore on the island of Mykonos. A tragedy. Then she moved inland with her father. She is his only child, a lovely girl."

"A sad story. Does she have a friend?"

"I watch these young people growing up, the aches and pains of the heart, and hear plenty of gossip from my customers and other fishermen." Pointing to the pile of nets, he said, "Life is complex, like these threads and knots. She is still young and naive about the ways of men; she has not sorted out her own heart."

"But whom does she favor?"

"In her village, there are three young lads who pursue her, but she is undecided. Anyway, her father is not ready to give her away."

Circe had satisfied her curiosity for now. She climbed up the steps and waved goodbye to the fishmonger, wishing him "a good day's catch."

Veering away from the promenade, she followed a couple of seagulls along the shore, and then rushed to the western slopes of Delos. For the rest of the day, she explored green patches of vegetation and foraged for the rare botanical specimens of the island, content to be alone in the outdoors. On Aeaea, she had studied and unraveled the secrets of Gaia, Mother Earth, and she applied the powers and magic of witchcraft and her knowledge of herbs.

There were no trails to follow. The rocky terrain was suitable for goats and rabbits. She briskly made her way up the hill and sat on a smooth rock, scanning the expanse of land and sea. Silver Delos was a diamond among the Aegean islands, yet she missed her own. Here she valued spending her days incognito, moving about among mortals, learning about their woes and joys, getting a closer glimpse of their lives. It was a window to Glaucus's past life as a fisherman.

She would have to find out more about his Boeotia island days tomorrow: What kind of sorcerer was he? When did he learn about herbs? How much did he know? Had he ever undertaken the onerous search to identify those growing on land? She could quiz him with questions about one plant she called "eye." To find it, one had to climb the mountain hunting for places where eagles build their nests—there, in the eagle's dung, the herb grows. It is a rare and precious herb, and chewing on a few leaves makes one's eyes sharp, like those of an eagle, able to track the slightest movement for miles around.

Then there is a root that can be found only near riverbanks. Its effects are permanent. The roots have to be rotten, chewed and spat by vermin. Those lucky enough to find them, by the giveaway tiny yellow flowers that grow wild, have to dry them for three months, keep them away from sunlight, and grind them to a fine powder. The grounds can be mixed in liquid or sprinkled on food. The unfortunate people who ingest it will misjudge most everything, making fools of themselves, making poor decisions. They will believe they are in love with people they loathe. They will hear the truth but believe it to be a lie. Consuming too much could lead to hallucinations and even blindness.

Perhaps he knew about some herbs, but not their opposites. Maybe he knew only about sea algae and other substances that live in the sea. There could be an opportunity for her to learn. Exciting common ground! She would have to find out. For now, she would choose a few plants that grow in Delos.

A tall shadow overtook her, accompanied by the distinct lavender perfume used by Perse. "Mother!" Circe spun around toward the woman approaching her from behind. "Must you always sneak up on me?" But the woman just smiled, like she always did, her black hair adorned with golden chains, her body graced by strings of amber necklaces and bracelets. Her radiant golden earrings, a gift from Helios, reflected the sun. She had embellished her turquoise tunic and himation with images of dolphins swimming between kelp swirls. She had tied a sash made from strings of pearls around her waist. Her blue eyes stayed on the sea when she spoke to her daughter.

"I wish you wouldn't do that," Circe said, frowning. It was rare that her mother arrived for a good reason. Always, there was that familiar disapproval—always some kind of problem to come meddle in. Pushing her curls away from her eyes, Circe's mother slipped a shawl around her body and turned to face her.

"At last, you've found a proper companion, an immortal! Don't mess it up this time, daughter," she said, her voice icy. "All your past relationships, especially your recent affair with Odysseus, were beneath your station. A mere mortal that already had a wife and son," she said, her voice dripping acid. "Only immortals are suitable for goddesses."

Perse moved closer and propped herself on a throne that she materialized with a flick of her hand. "And what is all this sleeping under the pines? A goddess needs servants, proper food, and a bed to rest. You are turning into a hermit. The temples will offer you all the services you are entitled to. I can intercede on your behalf."

Circe did not expect her to understand nor approve her ways. She held her mother's gaze for a moment before answering. "I am glad you like Glaucus. I am deeply attracted to him, want to know his story, and I have my ways to lure him." Silence followed. Then she rolled her eyes. "I don't need the services of the temple. I am a daughter of Nature, which has shared with me her secrets and given me my powers. And as for humans, they are precious, not just toys for the gods to play with. I enjoy getting to know them."

"Sometimes I think you are not my daughter, Circe. Still, I have one more piece of advice for you. You know a lot more and can teach him about potions and transformation, but he does not need to know about poisons."

A pause followed. Circe wondered: *Is she waiting to get some appreciation for her advice? I have none to give her.*

Besides, Circe found this to be odd advice, but her mother rarely made much sense to her. At least this time she would not get in her way, for—with an air of aggravation—Perse faded into the ether without further debate. Her mother gone, Circe burst out with anger and spit out her frustrations, waving her arms. "Who is she to try to give me advice about men? She never stops arguing with Father. Sometimes I don't know how he puts up with her." She looked around, wondering if her mother might be eavesdropping, but there was no sign. Relieved, she set out on her way up the slope, toward a clump of trees with thick underbrush. The hillside was quiet, much like her own island. Nearing the trees, she caught some movement on the ground. It was a lizard sprinting to hide. Circe followed it as it traversed its way under a rock. When she reached the spot, she gently raised the rock and found a rare species of mushroom growing underneath. She picked some carefully, one by one, and placed them in the satchel that hung on her side. She would test Glaucus to see if he recognized them.

In the middle of the thicket, she reached up to examine a cedar tree. She cut a small branch, removed some leaves, and rubbed them between her fingers to release their aroma. Her senses grew alert when she inhaled the pleasing fragrance. In the past, she had used them in an infusion that eased coughs. She added a handful to her satchel and stayed in the shade, avoiding the sun that had reached its zenith.

Circe sensed movement stirring inside a bleached deer's skull that lay on the clearing. A slithering shadow slipped from one of its eye holes, weaving its way through scrubby brush. A snake? She narrowed her eyes, but it kept approaching, impossibly long—longer than the snakes that glide around Aeaea. It was poisonous. It fattened and spilled, undulating across the dirt. Circe watched it for a brief time and then released a lightning spear that instantly killed it. It was still writhing when a passing eagle, immune to its poison, landed on the ground, ready to enjoy the incidental meal. *The way of the world*, Circe thought. *But Mother can no longer dominate my life. She presumes!*

That is part of her trouble. Why did she reveal my identity at the temple? She had spoiled her fun. From now on, she would try to avoid walking around the sanctuaries.

A few steps away, an unmistakable spread of wildflowers covered the dry soil, a species she had collected but had never used in the past. The large, lacy flowers that grew under the shade of a laurel were crowns of water hemlock, one of the most violently toxic plants she knew; its most potent poisons were stored in its roots. Ignoring her mother's warnings, Circe dug one out to carry with her so she could warn Glaucus about its properties, which caused convulsions and nausea, and often led to death. Shaking off the dirt, she wrapped the plant roots carefully in a handful of leaves from a sycamore tree and added the plant to her satchel.

Even on arid Delos, Gaia had sowed the land with riches, verdant patches that held her healing and dark powers, known only by the chosen ones. Powerful Circe venerated the earth. When she was admitted to the circle of Gaia's secrets and mysteries, she had gained the respect of the Olympians. Her meticulous studies had paid off and might bear more fruit when she got to know Glaucus better.

ELEVEN

C irce counted the days since her arrival in Delos. In another four, she wanted to be back on Aeaea to see Odysseus off. Every day was precious.

When she reached the promenade, she found the fishing boats preparing to go out after the evening catch. Some were heading to the steep shoreline with deep waters that was a perfect fishing spot; a couple were fishing with bait right from the boat dock. The fishmonger had already left for the open sea and was casting his nets. There was still plenty of daylight. The enchantress decided to leave the port and look for Skylla.

She began her trek. Starting from the familiar bay and teleporting over the main path, she skimmed over nearby villages until she ran into the boy she had met at the beach.

She landed by him and wasted no time. "Where does Skylla live?"

Upon seeing her, the lad shuffled back a step or two. Regaining his composure, he greeted her, "Circe!"

Obligingly he walked with her to the pasture next to Skylla's home, pointed out the house, and continued on his way. Passing by a couple of grazing cows, Circe cut through the grass and clover and approached the home, making herself invisible. It was dusk by the time she neared the fence and recognized the girl. Skylla was reclining in the yard, under a palm tree, a furry black dog curled up by her feet. It was a modest home close to the village well, neighboring a dairy farm.

Skylla's father, Phorkys, was a short, burly man with a slumped carriage, his hands strong and callused. He was busy stacking wood by the firepit inside the house when he heard a creature— perhaps it was an owl—screech in the distance. As he turned toward the hoot, he realized he had run out of feed for the chickens and needed some fish for their next meal. *How could I have forgotten that?* Outside, he stalled again, finding that his daughter had fallen asleep reading, and nudged her awake. "I am going to town to purchase supplies for tomorrow. Do you want to come along?"

The girl, still groggy, turned him down. He returned to the house to take up some coins and a bag to carry his purchases from the agora, then he set out on the road.

It was Circe who had sent him the shopping reminder, triggered by the owl's call. She waited and watched until he was beyond the pasture, on the main road to town. She knew it would take him an hour to reach his destination and another to return.

When he was out of sight, the enchantress made herself visible and walked up to the yard. A fence surrounded the house, built with rows of rocks, an anchor marking the center. Skylla's dog ran to Circe, her tail wagging. Seeing the goddess approach, the girl collected fallen sheets of paper from the ground, then straightened her tunic before welcoming Circe.

"You know how to read?"

"And write!" Skylla's face shone with pride. She picked up her dog, Aura, and held her, scratching her chin.

"Who is your teacher?"

"My father, Phorkys. He never denies me anything. I pestered him and he showed me how."

"You are a lucky girl." Circe smiled, pleased with the young woman's accomplishments. Only a handful of women would ever receive this kind of tutelage. Skylla set her dog down and invited Circe into their humble one-story home. They crossed the andron, a large room where they would welcome their rare male visitors, and entered the inner courtyard surrounded by columns. In the center was the marble altar of Zeus. As far as Circe could see, the rooms around the courtyard were tidy and the floors were covered with reed mats. All shutters were closed to keep the house cool. Skylla offered Circe a chair near the altar and brought out figs and honey from the storeroom.

Delicately tasting a fig, Circe looked around the home again and noticed the absence of a loom. "Where's your mother?" she asked.

The girl's face fell. It was a painful story, she said, her young mother dying shortly after childbirth. Skylla had been a motherless child, much loved by a father who had given up the seduction of sailing the seas in order to raise her.

"What about you?" She turned to the enchantress. "What brought you to Delos?"

There was an openness to the girl that led Circe to confide about her partnership with Odysseus that was about to end. "He's set on returning to his family."

Skylla's eyes widened at the name of the Trojan War hero. For a moment, she seemed stunned to silence.

"Your life is so rich, O Circe," she finally sighed. "I don't expect such honor, nor such grief as you have endured. My own future is simple, here in Delos: to become the wife of a man I will give my heart to."

"May the gods grant you a brilliant future." Circe turned

toward Mount Olympus. "And what about the boys you like? And how do you feel about Glaucus?"

Skylla's trusting voice ran on like water trickling down a merry brook, sharing all her innermost thoughts. "I especially like two local boys, but I have not settled who will have my heart. I am in no hurry to leave my father. He has had such a hard time and age has brought him health challenges, Circe." Her eyes moistened. "I will wait for as long as it takes, and when he is ready to give me away, I will choose between them. Please don't tell Glaucus about this."

Aura had approached Circe, demanding attention. The goddess smiled, reached down and rubbed the dog's belly, and then pressed her hand on Skylla's arm to reassure her. "Your secret is safe with me. But why is it you want to keep this from Glaucus?"

"He would be jealous of my love for my father and the boy I choose. I do not know why he seeks my attention. He is at my beach waiting for me every day!"

Circe felt as though a knife had pierced her heart. She looked away, biting down on her bottom lip. But the girl was still speaking.

"Thank you for listening. I have no one to share my thoughts with, Circe." Skylla rested trusting eyes on the enchantress.

"He is in love with you," Circe said and remembered Aristos's words. *Still young and naive about the ways of men*, he'd told her, *she has not sorted out her own heart.* And it was true: Circe felt a sudden streak of envy for the young woman.

"I am trying my best to dissuade his affection!" the girl responded. "But his knowledge of algae has been so helpful. He knows a lot about algae. I bring some home because they help my father. Especially red algae. I use them to help his digestion."

Silence followed for several moments. Circe was impressed. "Nature is a wonderful doctor, worth studying. Does your father have other ailments?"

"He has pain in his joints and his knees are swollen," she answered, twisting her hair mechanically. "I worry about him."

"I may be able to help." With that, Circe thanked the young woman for her hospitality and bade her goodnight. The girl's indifference to Glaucus was a relief. It was time for Circe to try her best to find out if there was any hope for a relationship with the amphibian. She still was a sorceress; she had many guiles. It was urgent to plot her strategy for the next morning.

She spent a lot of her night under the pines anxiously preparing to astonish him in the morning. There had been no one she desired who had escaped her flirtation before. Glaucus had been easy to engage in dance. He was responsive, a showman who liked grand arrivals and departures. Attractive as she was, she dreamed of how she might make a star appearance when they met again.

She shut her eyes and visualized garments she could conjure up for the next day. Her best tunic would be purple, made of silk, fit for a queen, and she would have a sash made of seashells. She would add a light himation to drape over the tunic, one adorned with semiprecious stones and a golden meander along its seams. On her hair she would fasten precious beads and would carry her satchel with the precious gifts from the slopes of Delos.

Should she come riding on a horse when he arrived at the rock? Or would that be too extravagant? Her smile would be bright, and she would glow and shimmer like a creature of the sea. She might even shed her clothes, join him in the water; he would admire her slender body and their hello would be a passionate joining of voluptuous lips—that should fire up his desire for a woman. And she would look young, even younger than Skylla, for him tomorrow.

Would he see her coming down from heaven to be with him, or would he turn away? Would he stay with her? Would he be charmed, or would he vanish?

TWELVE

Glaucus considered where to swim that evening to collect young, tender algae growing around the lip of a neighboring caldera for Circe. She was an intriguing woman, attractive, willing to dive into the sea for adventure, and most famous for her mastery of the secrets of land herbs. Only a chosen few had spent days and months delving into this study, among them Hippocrates, well known for employing their medicinal properties. The chance to learn and share had piqued his interest. The algae he gathered had to be special. It was his way of showing hospitality and appreciation for her visit. He was drawn to a variety suspended in the water, no more than six inches in height, distinct for its golden-brown color and velvety feel.

The search only briefly took his mind off Skylla, a mere mortal, even though her disregard of him made him angry. The girl was a puzzle. The virgin Delian beauty had conquered his heart: her youth, lanky body, budding breasts, long hair, curvy lines, gorgeous heart-shaped lips he yearned to kiss. He had not managed to touch her yet. She evaded him every time he sought her out. He had approached her by the rock, in shallow water, and in the deep sea swirling around her gently, always careful not to frighten her.

"Skylla, you are truly a creature of the sea. I love how you swim, dive, and play in the water," he had told her. For a long time, he had synchronized his swimming next to her, keeping the same speed and talking about the wonders of the fathomless sea. "In the kingdom of mighty Poseidon, I have found worlds richer than those on land. There is life eternal, brighter than the galaxies, busier than the promenade of Delos, more precious than gold. Come," he had urged her, reaching to take her hand, but she slipped away.

"I am a creature of the land, Glaucus," she occasionally objected, but she mostly ignored him.

He knew why he was so attracted to Skylla. It was not just her beauty, her youth and innocence. Although he extolled life in the sea, he missed human companionship and wanted her loyalty. His sea neighbors, the Nereids, were fluid, fancy-free, and changing partners all the time. He yearned for her devotion, just like what she felt for her father. He needed a wife.

Carrying algae, he returned to the gathering of nymphs busy gossiping about the latest adventures of Odysseus. "He hopes to talk to Tiresias in Hades, but all these other ghosts want to drink the blood he offered in sacrifice. Will the old seer speak to him?" asked Erato, the oldest Nereid, looking for more recent developments.

"Circe sent him there, and now she is roaming Delos. Is she trying to get rid of him?" said the youngest one, who was ready to part with her own lover.

"You are always looking for ways to ditch your lovers," Glaucus said, approaching the gathering. The other nymphs tittered merrily.

The young one did not realize how transparent she had been to the others. She shied away from them, but not before making a pitiful remark. "And you are hopelessly chasing after Skylla. Poor Glaucus!" Then she fled.

Glaucus did not care for her. He had befriended her lover, a young amphibian, sweet and considerate of the Nereid and yet unsuccessful, just like himself. He admired this fellow's patience.

He waved her away, creating turbulence with his tail in her direction. His features tight, he moved away from the nymphs. He did not care for their gossipy chatter. His thoughts returned to Skylla. There were times he wanted to overpower her, willfully take her to the dark kingdom with him; other times he was so frustrated that he had nearly abandoned his pursuit, but only for a day. There was no other for him.

Best to focus on gathering herbs for the visiting goddess. She was a fine diversion. In the past, he had loved delving back into the ancient arts. Perhaps he could refocus and add another herb for the morning meeting with Circe. What could he offer that she might find useful on land?

That's when he remembered the herb he had consumed that made him immortal. He could tell her exactly where to find it on his natal home, the island of Boeotia. Since then, he had discovered another rare specimen with similar properties: granting eternal youth to the receiver. It was in the deep bottom of the sea, prickly, thorny, and hard to handle. It had wounded his fingers when he tried to pry it loose. He vaguely remembered where it was and thrust his body forward, propelled by his powerful tail toward the far corner of the island.

There he dove a thousand leagues below and searched for the precious bush. In the cold, dark waters he passed by oddly shaped sea creatures, swimming close to the sandy bottom, inside fields of rock and coral. He slowed down when he came upon a shipwreck and dove into the storage bowels of the ship; it was still loaded with transport amphorae: large clay jars that once held wine and other liquids. It likely had sunk because the weather was not always temperate in that part of the Aegean. Lives lost. Yearning for his days on land pulled him in to inspect the row of amphorae.

Eons ago, he had been an ordinary mortal, a fisherman. He, too, had purchased wine from a ship like this that had carried it from the harbor of Thassos island. There were simple pleasures in his old life: fishing, his boat, his hut, and an occasional glass of wine with friends. He could have traveled to Delos; he could have met Skylla then. Finding the moly that gave him eternal life was a blessing and a curse. Any creature, man or amphibian, is never satisfied. Neither are gods.

Realizing that dawn was approaching, he worried he might miss Skylla today. That would not do, but he was disoriented. He changed direction twice, beat the bottom of the sea with his mighty tail, raising a cloud of sand, and shook his head in disappointment. Glancing around, he realized it was time to call for help. He prayed to his protector, kneeling by a bed of coral: "Beloved master of the seas, I beseech you to send me a guide, for I have taken too long wandering and don't remember where to look." And he waited.

Had Poseidon heard him? Would he indulge him? Moving through a dense forest of pale-fringed kelp, he waited. Hundreds of small fish sprang away, disturbed by his presence. An odd-shaped monster appeared and circled him. It was round, with bulging eyes, thorny fins, and dark skin—but a gentle creature. Glaucus clutched its tail and together they swam to yet darker waters, deeper than the distance to the top of Kilimanjaro, to depths the sun could not penetrate. The monster led him close to the entrance of a cave and stopped next to a plentiful clump of living limbs waving in the water innocently. Glaucus recognized the plant immediately; he released the monster and swam around it to find the best approach.

He reached out to touch it, testing how deeply it was rooted in the seabed. An oozing milky liquid clouded the waters and stung his eyes. Giving up the notion to tear it up, he took out his knife and carefully carved a cone segment, approaching it from above. Then he guided the chunk to a box he had carried with him just for this purpose. It was a special box made of abalone shell he had fashioned himself. It would be a gift to Circe, a souvenir from Glaucus and Delos. A precious gift.

THIRTEEN

The restless enchantress, swept away by her passion but uncertain about how to approach the next day, conjured up scenarios that she would discard, starting over with new ones. What if she appeared on the shore wearing a simple tunic, or what if she hovered swimming near the rock carrying the herbs she had collected? What if she sent Skylla away? Perhaps she should join Skylla for a swim and observe Glaucus's reaction with her own eyes. She tossed and turned all night. Morning found her short of sleep.

Fully awakened by Skylla's arrival, she checked the water for rippling waves around the formidable rock—but no Glaucus yet. She watched the young woman shed her clothes by the bushes and move into the sea. She was attractive! Circe took stock of her own charms, still confident about her appeal and flirting skills. It should be easy to attract Glaucus, especially knowing that Skylla had no interest in him. Daytime casts a different light on the world.

In the end, discarding the fancy wardrobe ideas, a youthful and energetic Circe joined Skylla for a morning swim. It was a gorgeous, sunny day with Helios reigning in all his majesty over the calm, warm waters of the bay. The two women were still swimming when Glaucus appeared by the rock. With the usual splash and thunder, he emerged from the depths and waited for them to come near. Circe smiled with satisfaction. All signs were good.

As the two women swam together, Circe said, "It will be an exchange between Glaucus and me, meant for immortals only, not of interest to you, Skylla. Go on with your day."

Clearly eager to agree, Skylla responded with a sigh of relief and a nod.

Circe noticed the moment Glaucus lost his smile. He had been following them with his eyes as they reached the shore. He realized Skylla had grabbed her clothes and hurried toward the path to the village. "Good day, Skylla! You are leaving us?" He scowled.

Circe, who had quickly applied stardust on her body, said, "To give us time to talk. Wait for me a minute longer while I dry my hair." She had noticed the abalone shell box he held. Pointing to it, she asked, "You bring me gifts, Glaucus? You remembered? I have some as well. Let me get my satchel. I'll be right there." She did not bother to dress. All along she'd thought, *Today has to be the day I charm Glaucus.*

For the next hour, Circe stuck to a conversation about herbs and their potential uses. She watched him relax into the discussion. Besides, she was especially thrilled with the rare contents of the box. Granting immortality was a power only gods had held up until then. She thanked him profusely when he advised her to preserve the plant by keeping it covered in seawater in the abalone shell box. In her assessment, his knowledge in the dark arts was quite shallow, but he had mastered resources of the sea and this gift was superb.

She taught him about the properties of cedar and the crowns of water hemlock, but he seemed most interested in the mushrooms. What was fascinating about them was that depending on the amount used, they could have opposite effects: a small amount healed with its powerful antioxidant effects, but a large amount poisoned, transforming a human into disturbing forms. She had used it to turn Odysseus's sailors to pigs.

Circe drenched her voice in honey and changed the conversation: "I praise Aphrodite, whose shafts of light are sheet silver that shimmer on your body. I am so pleased to be with you, handsome Glaucus, and learn about your world." She batted her long eyelashes.

"You are a truly beautiful woman, Circe," he complimented her.

Was she getting somewhere? She reached into her satchel for her velvety red lipstick, touched up her cheeks and mouth using the water for a mirror, puckered her lips, and looked up directly into his eyes. "Do you see something you want?"

Glaucus blinked. "You have lovely eyes," he started, then paused, apparently not understanding what she wanted from him.

Circe could hear the discomfort in his voice. Was he fearful of intimacies? He seemed so tuned to Skylla. Was he just being polite, clumsy? Circe, still tingling with excitement, enveloped him with a seductive look and lightly stroked his hair.

"Don't look at me like that!" Glaucus pulled back.

Surging red, Circe turned away, and an awkward silence followed. He broke it first. "There are rites the Nereids and I perform, sacred rites revealing the secrets of death and rebirth in life and nature. Perhaps you would like to join us tonight?" She was unable to reply, so he continued, "These rites are for protection, meant to appease the gods, to give supplicants safe passage to what they seek, always under the protection of Poseidon. Do you want to join us, Circe?"

Still struggling to recover, she said, "Your company is enough for me tonight, dear Glaucus. We share so much! Thank you for inviting me." Had she scared him?

"I am grateful for the gifts you have given me," he said. "No one else had contributed to my knowledge before. I could bring you another kind of algae that is useful and plentiful here— tomorrow, if you are still here?"

"Could I follow you to where you find the algae? I would like to know what their habitat is like." She recalled their first meeting, the dance, the dreamy exchange that had ignited her hopes. Perhaps he would be more relaxed in his liquid element.

He nodded agreement, pointed in a direction, and moved ahead of her. Circe covered her body with a tight silver coat of scalelike skin and followed him into the cooler, darker blue waters. He moved fast. Making an enormous effort, she caught up with him, panting and reaching for his fin. "Looking for a ride," she called out, though when he turned to see what it was about, she smiled calmly again, watching his eyes rest upon her breasts.

"I like your outerwear shift," he said politely, resuming his course and inviting her to hold on. They traveled well into deeper water until they'd reached the sea floor. She walked first along a depression, then a mound of sand to see beyond it a bright opening to the garden of the Nereids. It was a vast, luscious paradise, a park unlike any she had seen. Vibrant sea flowers—purple, yellow, and pink, in constant motion—were scattered on a clump of rocks. Then came arbors of feather-leaved sea-plants and tall strings of kelp, gently dancing, forming fencing and pathways, as far as the eye could see. And there was more life: small- and medium-sized fish and octopi, seahorses and turtles. Glaucus smiled at the Nereid approaching them and said to the sorceress, "This is one place where most all varieties of algae thrive. Here live my friends, the Nereids."

Circe straightened her carriage, boosted her breasts, pursed her lips, and declared, "I wouldn't mind living in this paradise."

"And who is your guest?" the Nereid asked him, holding a baby dolphin in her arms, bottle-feeding it milk.

"Erato, this is famous Circe, daughter of Helios and Perse."

"Welcome, Circe, to our world." She was a sociable, inquiring Nereid and the two had a pleasant exchange. Circe praised

71

Delos and its waters, giving a full report about what she had enjoyed on land during her visit. From Erato, she learned that the garden harbored babies of many species. There were crawling crabs, seahorses, and sea turtles near them. Glaucus picked up a couple of sea turtles and held them in his palm for her to see. Pleased, Circe tittered like a child, hugging Glaucus lightly, ignoring the watchful eyes of the Nereid.

The three moved deeper into the garden. A small group of curious Nereids went by and nodded their hellos. Circe noticed all the curious eyes and loudly admired the world they had created. It was Poseidon's wish for his nymphs to be surrounded by beauty.

Glaucus told Erato he would take Circe to the garden of algae, and the two moved on. This was her chance. Threading her arm under his fin, she raised the unspoken questions she had been harboring. "Glaucus, do you remember what it was like to shape-shift after taking the moly?" She still carried the powerful memory of her dream before she ever met him, the sensation of awe, and expected him to share a revelation, an experience intense and mystical, perhaps even painful. Would he share it? She felt his body stiffen as he stopped steering them forward.

"No one has asked that before. But there isn't much to say." He laughed nervously.

"How did the moly affect you, Glaucus?" Circe pressed.

He looked uncertain but responded hurriedly: "A numb feeling and achy muscles. A momentary panic when I lost my balance. But Poseidon lifted me right then to his watery kingdom."

"Were you scared?"

"Of course not!"

How could he not be? Was he shutting the door? She was quiet, disappointed. Was he, after all, shallow and mistrusting?

72

She started a new line of inquiry. "What family did you have in Boeotia?"

"An old story." After a long pause, he asked shyly, "Are you sure you want to hear it?"

Her sharp nod answered him. She was used to getting her answers and spoke in a commanding voice. "I bid you to proceed."

He sighed. "Everyone seems to know about my past, so you might as well know too. My mother raised me single-handedly because my father was a drunk and incapable of work. I have always loved the sea. I learned how to fish to help put food on the table. She worked for a rich household that allowed her to bring me along when I was an infant. A hard life."

"Parents have troubles of their own," she answered, thinking about her arrogant mother, her busy, unavailable father, Helios, and her parents' frequent bickering. Then she asked, "Did you have a wife, children?"

"Yes, a wife and a son. Innocents I had to abandon since I shifted form. The Fates took good care of them."

"Do you think of them?"

"Rarely."

At first, his answer surprised her. It had to be his infatuation with Skylla that faded his attachment to them, she decided.

"It was a long time ago," he answered pensively.

They had reached the algae garden. For her, it was like entering a dense forest in dark waters. The tall algae were two lengths of her. She loved pushing through branches and followed him quietly. Holding on to his fin, she feigned fear that she might lose him in the thick brush. He led the way to a delicate garden of light green algae with feathered edging. Several limbs stretched out of the tall bushes that seemed to resist touch. He reached for a branch and the plant retreated. He tried again, finally getting a firm hold on a branch. He cut a snippet with his knife, twirling it around with his fingers and handing it to her to examine.

"This is what I was after," he said. "You want to keep only the lacy ends. It has magical qualities. Chewing on it can break a fever. We use it in Poseidon's sacred rites to demonstrate the two ways of being: passive and energetic. The visual impact is powerful when the initiates witness a sickly person fully recover and take charge of his life. Revealing and using its properties brings many converts to our cult."

Circe examined the slice, bringing it close to her skin, then her eyes, still bothered by Glaucus's businesslike tone. Sensing that she was losing her grip on him again, she felt herself wax impatient. "Can I keep it?" she retorted, drawing the sample back away from her nose. He nodded, so she pushed further. "I am getting tired. Can we return to the island?"

"I have to attend to a ceremony of Poseidon's rites very soon. So I won't be able to accompany you all the way. At the gate, Poseidon's messenger will be waiting to take you back to land."

"Will I see you again tomorrow?" Her voice was going stark. How was it he could resist her charms so fully?

"Most likely. I hope this was worthwhile for you. But if I don't see you, have a pleasant stay on Delos."

They soon parted. She came away preoccupied with all that had unfolded on this intense, complicated day.

FOURTEEN

As soon as Circe had set off, following her dolphin guide, a scrum of Nereids descended on Erato to quiz her about the visitor. A gifted storyteller, she gave them a vivid account of the exchange. She was especially struck with the enchantress's declaration about "living in this paradise" and her seductive appearance in fishlike outerwear that they all had witnessed. "Friendly enough, agreeable and touring Delos, but is really after Glaucus and visits the rock every day." She giggled and rolled her eyes. "Circe may be exploring the island, pleasing the gods with sacrifices, meeting the priests, with the thought of moving here. It's too early to tell. And Glaucus is clueless!"

The Nereids joined in, eager to share their impressions. They filled the huddle with three names: "Circe . . . Glaucus . . . Skylla . . . Glaucus . . ."

"Imagine," one said, "each day at the break of dawn, sitting at the rock. It certainly tells me she is after him. Did you see how she looked at him?"

"Doesn't she realize that Glaucus is interested in Skylla? It's plain to see."

"That was a sexy outfit she had on. Glaucus could see all her parts," Pandora, another Nereid, commented, wiggling provocatively as if imitating Circe's walk. "She was shimmering like his own amphibian body. What was that about?"

"You are jealous," her friend teased, and the others clapped enthusiastically.

Annoyed, she responded, "I think Circe wants him to replace Odysseus."

Erato knew their chatter would keep them busy for a while. She demanded: "Don't you have chores to take care of?" Erato took charge, as she usually did, even though she knew it was an annoying habit to the rest of them. Leaving the swarm to search for Glaucus, she muttered, "I wonder what Glaucus has to say about Circe."

She found him in the garden of sacred rites, where a ceremony was in progress, with Glaucus assisting the high priest. She watched the proceedings silently from the sidelines, her face reverent and downcast so as not to disturb the initiates.

The high priest, dressed in silver-and-blue regalia, chanted a hymn he dedicated to Poseidon. He blessed those in attendance, a small crowd of tritons, Nereids, and divers, all of whom had bowed their heads, and then asked Glaucus to distribute the algae he had collected to each one present. His final guidance to all was to track and record their dreams that night and bring them in for the next gathering. Finally, he assured them that each dream revealed a kernel of truth, one that they would benefit from knowing. And with that, the initiates started to disperse.

When Glaucus had finished with his duties, Erato joined him, returning to the main garden. They could hear one of the Nereids strumming eerie tunes of the deep sea on her kithara.

"You brought an interesting guest today. No one expected that," Erato said, tilting her head.

Glaucus made no reply.

"Did you see how she looked at you?"

"How was that?"

"Oh, her eyes, my dear, her pulsing body. Can't you recognize a woman in love?" She said it with a knowing smile and then scolded him. "A goddess is in love with you, Glaucus, and all you want is that mortal girl."

"Stay out of it, Erato. I love Skylla. Horses would have to gallop on the ocean floor and fish would have to climb to the top of mountains before I stop loving her." He glared at Erato, his voice hoarse.

But the Nereid could see what he was not saying aloud: he was reduced to a begging pauper, bent on his knees for alms from Skylla. Did her heart have none to give? The name suited her well: *bitch!*

He turned away abruptly and swam fast, leaving her behind. Erato's warning words followed: "You had better tell Circe that the one you love is Skylla, then."

Glaucus was too riled up to sleep. Even without his tormenting thoughts of Skylla, his fascination with the new herbs and their potential powers was enough to keep him awake, especially the mysterious mushroom that held both good and evil. He remembered Circe's warning about what amounts to use, the need to measure the dose proportionate to the weight of the receiver. He reached into his pouch for one and delicately placed it on his palm; it was small in size, light brown with red spots on its cap. He lifted his finger and touched the cap. The sting he felt on his face was immediate, coming from the milky liquid it released that clouded the waters. For a moment, he felt his heart seizing. He pulled his body away and carefully returned the mushroom to the pouch.

He could give Skylla a precious mouthful of the sea herbs he had saved in his own abalone shell box and gift her eternal life—if she only loved him. He did not care (he shook his head again and again) for eternal life—only for her mortal love—and yet he had been given eternity to torture his heart! His days had been poisoned. He could see how gods, power, and religions trade in good and evil. He felt his own power, for he could also end his torment by poisoning her with the mushrooms, and be done!

But could Erato's usually perceptive eyes be right? Another woman! All Circe was to him was a wiser colleague, protected by Poseidon—no more. Although their dance on the day they met delighted him and she had hinted that she loved this garden and could live in it, that had to be more about her admiration of the garden. Yet it would not hurt to follow Erato's advice.

FIFTEEN

*I*n the aftermath of her visit to the garden, Circe thought over all that had passed that day. She sought the advice of her Nana, but met only silence. She would have to trust her own intuition, as she had done all her life. Her night was restless; she spent it walking around the temples, which were quiet in the absence of people. It was her way of centering, listening to her inner guidance. But not tonight. She remained indecisive.

When the threesome met again, at the usual spot and the usual time, Skylla greeted the other two and prepared for her swim. Circe and Glaucus stayed by the rock, conversing about the beauty of the garden and all its mysteries. The minute that Glaucus realized Skylla had swum away without another word to them, he arched his body. "Look at how she is ignoring me!" An enormous wave splashed the rock following the angry twitch of his tail.

Circe waited for the foam to settle. "I am not ignoring you, dear Glaucus." She spoke in her sweetest voice, her dimples deepening. "Which of us is fairer?"

She saw she had startled him. Did he not recognize the contest between the two women? Perhaps he did now, for his face reddened and he stammered, "Circe, I have a favor to ask. Could I have one of your love potions? It is for Skylla. I am desperate to gain her affection."

Circe froze. After a moment, she said in a chilled voice, "I don't believe you need a potion, Glaucus. Just tell her how you feel about her."

Then she turned away to hide the anger that seared her face. How could she be so torn, more by resentment of him than jealousy of that simple girl? Her heart ached; her pride was shredded. After all her trouble to seek him out, this is what she got? Bested by a mortal? Already, she could hear Perse's savage laughter ridiculing her.

What's worse, Glaucus was clearly living in a dream world, blind to the sorceress's presence, her beauty and attraction to him. He was willing to connive to capture a heart that was not his. In her eyes, the gentle amphibian was losing his charm.

"But she knows," came his simple answer.

Lovelorn and blind! she thought. "Genuine love does not come from potions, Glaucus. Besides, I would not interfere."

It was a clear defeat, one she had never encountered in her life. She needed to collect her thoughts. Excusing herself, Circe mumbled that they expected her at the harbor. She didn't even care if he knew she was lying.

But Circe, for all her sorcery and fame, felt an unaccustomed despair. Hollowed by rejection, she felt the dark worms of humiliation eating away at her soul, and her resentment built further each time she spied on them and witnessed Glaucus's adoration for Skylla. Yet she liked the girl, an innocent caught up in webs woven by immortals. Circe took the long way, walking to the harbor. Her fury was settling into more rumination about her situation. She hated to give up and despised giving her mother an opportunity to put her down one more time. But was her mother's opinion worth all that pain? Why did it still matter? She was no longer a child. Perhaps the fishmonger would be there to amuse her. Maybe it was time to return to Aeaea?

By now, the harbor was busy with two large ships unloading cargo from the mainland. Delian merchants were bidding for the goods, and there was a flurry of activity with porters unloading the sold merchandise. She could see Hermes watching the humans' preoccupation with the acquisition of goods. It was his kind of day.

Coming to Aristos's boat, she found him resting on the forward thwart and greeted him fondly. "I will miss talking with you, Ariste."

"Are you leaving us, O goddess?"

"Soon," she said, taking a deep look at him, storing his image in her memory. His wrinkles were deep from the hard sun, his shoulders had drooped, but there was a softness to his eyes, a kindness to his smile. He was a likeness of the priest she had met at Poseidon's temple, except he had not grown a beard.

"Were you ever in love?"

"Once in love and another time infatuated," he said, smiling.

"You are wise to tell them apart."

"I have learned to tune in and yield to the tides of the sea."

She handed him a small box with salves she had made from cedar leaves and said, "A gift for you to use to soothe your sore joints at the end of the day."

That night, Circe had her answer about her aspirations of love and conquest in a dream she recognized to be all about choices and decisions. In her sleep, she was taken back to her familiar forest hut, back in Aeaea. She saw herself eagerly working on a deadly potion, in the moonlight, in her ceremonial garments, a long purple tunic belted with star- and moon-shaped stones. Her silver crown was fastened in her hair, sending pale halos of soft rays. In the pale light, she searched the shelves and chose three containers: one with roots and two with tree branches she had collected, dried, and stored. With a mortar and pestle, she mixed even amounts of leaves and pounded them into a fine powder. Then she took a knife and quartered a long gnarly root, dicing one piece for the brew. Measuring carefully with a cup, she added these ingredients to the cauldron.

The last touch was to add dried bat wings and a mysterious dark liquid to the cauldron, observing what effect it had. Then she added more liquid and watched the brew turn deep purple. She took a whiff to test the potency. It was right. Then she filled a goblet and handed it to the priest, the one she had met at Poseidon's temple in Delos, who was standing by. They were to start a procession. Facing them was a fork in the road. She knew that one path led to destruction, termination, the end of life, but she did not know which one.

The priest, his likeness to the fishmonger startling, wore garments fashioned for funeral services, a white tunic and black himation. His carriage was upright, his eyes piercing the horizon ahead. She handed him the silver goblet containing the potion and waited. The priest took it and bowed to her. His lips moved in prayer as he walked to the cauldron and slowly poured the potion back in.

She followed him into the forest with an open heart. Revenge was not to be. What a newfound relief . . .

SIXTEEN

The day after that disastrous meeting by the rock, Circe resolved to ask Poseidon for an escort back to Aeaea. There was the usual buzz of visitors at the Propylaea to Apollo's temple, and all along the Sacred Way, locals and travelers filled the shops and sanctuaries. The enchantress moved through the shoppers, purchased some sage, and approached Poseidon's temple, where a crowd had circled around someone important. There was no missing her overdressed and perfumed mother, speaking with the temple priests, all three of them gossiping with stories about the Olympians and their squabbles. Circe knew that her mother thrived when she was the center of attention. She also knew she had to prepare to endure another attack.

Temple staff recognized her and made room for her to walk inside. There were gentle torches lighting the interior, shedding affable yellow tongues on the walls. She approached the statue of majestic Poseidon, stirring waves with his trident, surrounded by gentle dolphins awaiting his commands. Lighting the sage, she purified the space around the god's statue, walked around it three times, and then dropped to her knees. She shut her eyes and focused her mind on delivering a grateful meditation for her time in Delos. She knew he would receive her prayer best this way, in a quiet praise to his might. There was a lot to be thankful for: the clarifying dream, his protection during her stay, and the escorts that had carried her. She ended her devotion by asking for his help for a safe return to Aeaea.

Just as she rose to walk outside the colonnade, Perse appeared at her elbow, regal and ferocious, her eyes steely and rapacious. For a long moment, she looked around the temple, finally fixing her eyes on Circe. "My daughter, a beautiful failure." Her spite was like nails, and they hit their target.

Circe's answer came slowly. "He was taken and not worthy, Mother." She paused. "You knew all along about Skylla, didn't you?" Her voice had turned curt and hurt.

"Of course I knew. A sorceress who refuses to use her own powers! You are a sad case, useless, defeated. You wasted another opportunity to show your craft." Put-downs—that was what her mother did best.

"It was not the time to show my craft. It was time to see reality and follow my intuition."

"You have wasted the only time an immortal crossed your path!" Perse hammered on.

Circe let loose a sigh, taking her time on the exhale, and folded her arms to her chest. "Can you ever respect and support my decisions, Mother?"

"You embarrass me, Circe. I am done defending your misadventures. Go back to your exile. You deserve it." Abruptly she dissolved into thin air, leaving a bitter cloud behind, and once more tarnishing their relationship.

Circe crept away quietly, feeling more alone than ever yet yearning for the isolation and the safety of her remote island. She still was the enchantress who could create powerful shifts of transformation, change a mouse to a lion, a bird to a warrior; she could kill with a word and heal wounds with salves. This time her heart was her guide, and although bruised, she knew this was the right course.

That night, she waited for all to leave, then curled up on a mat in the shade of Poseidon's statue, hoping to get a sign that her protector had listened to her request. But none came. She smudged the space with sage to cleanse it of her mother's residuum, and settled for the night.

The chasm between them was getting deeper. Her father seemed too busy to engage in her life; riding his chariot each morning to begin the day was his source of pride and gained him the people's reverence. He was clearly more interested in his relationship with the other gods than in his family. But her mother had no tasks to occupy her time, other than attending to her looks and whims. Why couldn't she love her? She was her youngest daughter.

Odysseus was on her mind too. He was due back any day now from his journey into the shadows of Hades. She wondered about Tiresias's prophecies and Odysseus's new plans, for he would have some to carry out. Then there was Elpinikis, the crew, and their preparations for the journey. Most of all, she missed foraging around her island, the company of her wild and friendly animals—lions and lambs alike, and her loom waiting for a new tapestry depicting the paradise gardens of the Nereids and perhaps even Glaucus and Erato.

The hoot of an owl in the night was like a message from Athena. It came from a nearby cave she could see on the next hill in the dim light of the moon. Perhaps the gods were deciding her fate. She trusted in Poseidon. After all, he had responded to all her prayers. He might send her a sign about her departure, but she still had one more stop to make.

The next morning, she woke up from a restful sleep to the sounds of people returning to the sanctuaries. Stepping out of the temple, she wrapped herself in a bright yellow himation to greet her father, the sun, who was breaking a brilliant sunrise on the horizon. A light breeze played in the pleats of her tunic

and himation, fanning it out majestically. She was radiating the
felicity she felt in her core.

She walked along the shore enjoying the stretch of it, sending grateful goodbyes to the rocks, the sand, the continuous
musings of the waves, and all the small creatures that nes-
tled along the beach—barnacles, crabs, and shells carried out
onshore—Poseidon's miracles.

Arriving at the rock beach just as Skylla was getting ready
for her swim, Circe settled in the shade of the pines and
watched her remove the ribbons from her hair and stretch her
limber limbs. What would unfold in her life? Her sympathy for
Skylla and her family had brought her back for one last time.
When she called her, the girl beamed and ran to settle by her
feet.

"The sea keeps you strong and lovely, Skylla." She admired
the young woman's beauty and vitality, still feeling a tiny pang
of jealousy.

"Since you arrived, no one has come to seek Glaucus's
advice. We are grateful to have the beach to ourselves," the girl
answered.

"They will return again. I have kept them away, but it is time
for life to take its usual course," said Circe. Then she handed
her a small box. "You are a dutiful daughter, Skylla. This is for
your father's sore joints. Apply this salve every morning. It will
relieve the pain and swelling."

Touched and thankful, Skylla reached out with her arms
open to show her appreciation. "You have been good to us,
Circe. Thank you. I want to learn more about herbs. Maybe
someday you will teach me."

"You are on the path already. Keep searching." It was the
hour of goodbyes. Circe was ready for her home. "I have loved
visiting Delos. I have learned a lot on your silver island, but it
is time to return home, before the rains."

Skylla joined her palms as if in prayer. "I will miss you, my goddess. Will you come back to see us again?"

Circe hedged, "Who knows what the Fates have in store? I follow my heart where it takes me. I know you do too." She wanted to say more about Glaucus, love, the dangers and the opportunities ahead, but she restrained herself. "I want to keep up with you. To send me messages, tap your right foot three times and call my name," she said.

Circe wrapped the lass in an envelope of protection and held her gaze affectionately. That was her last gift. A journey into the unknown was about to move everyone to discover their tomorrows. Who is to say what is to come?

"Goodbye, my dear," she said, and vanished.

SEVENTEEN

*I*t turns out some gods on Mount Olympus had been following Circe's adventures. She was the subject of a discussion that sprang up unexpectedly between Zeus, the father of all gods and men; Poseidon, master of the seas; Apollo, the gifted god of music and dance; and Athena, the wise daughter of Zeus. It was a slow news day on the mountain. There were no wars, no bloody disputes, no vendettas for gods to argue about. The mountain was clear with snow covering the nearby peaks.

Zeus surveyed the gathering, set his thunderbolts to the side of his throne and, with a slight wave of his hand, signaled his eagle companions to rest. Poseidon, his brother, and Apollo, his son, were huddled together with his daughter, Athena, by the eternal fire kept lit up day and night.

At daybreak, Apollo was playing dice with Poseidon, bending over the golden round table built by Hephaistos, the master craftsman, for their games. He had decorated the pedestal base with artfully sculpted shapes of two eagles. The two competitors dotted the morning with war cries announcing good rolls, poor moves, and victories. Each tossed the dice onto the table-top with gusto. Poseidon was barely ahead when he announced to the gathering, "Circe is ready to return to Aeaea, but I am in no hurry to get her back."

Zeus suppressed the urge to roll his eyes. It was hardly a secret that his brother was no fan of Odysseus. It annoyed the father of all that this attitude kept his brother from offering a helping hand to the homesick king of Ithaca who was trying to return to his family. Zeus glanced at Athena, knowing that she was eavesdropping and would have an opinion.

For a moment longer Athena continued sipping her ambrosia from a goblet in the shape of an owl. Her father had observed that ever since the end of the Trojan War, she had been tracking and protecting Odysseus from the dangers of the sea. "But Odysseus's ship is two days away from landing on Circe's island," she said. "Shouldn't we make sure she is back to see him off to Ithaca?" She turned to her father. "What do you think, Father Zeus?"

The father of all lightly rubbed his forehead but waited to give Poseidon a chance to overcome his mulish nature.

"My dolphins need to rest," grumbled Poseidon at last. "They are running an errand, and it is not done yet. Circe has to wait." His tone was nonnegotiable, and he tossed the dice again. It was a bad roll.

Apollo's face lit up with this favorable turn in his luck. With a big smile, he said to his uncle, "If I lose this game, I wager to give you that aulos you have always admired, shaped like a pair of razor clams, but if you lose, you should send another team of dolphins to Circe right away."

Poseidon stared at him for a long minute.

"It sounds like a good offer," interjected Zeus, who disliked Poseidon's stubborn ways. "Circe is ready to return. We will receive more prayers and sacrifices from a satisfied Circe and a grateful Odysseus."

Finally Poseidon nodded acceptance to the challenge and rolled the dice.

Whether because of Zeus's interference or Poseidon's poor luck, the roll of the dice was in Apollo's favor.

Satisfied with the outcome, Zeus took charge of the

moment. "Apollo wins, but my eagle will get her home faster than your dolphins, Poseidon."

No one dared cross him when he spoke. And it was done. Within the hour, he dispatched an eagle to Delos to find Circe.

But Zeus knew well the threat his brother's temper presented. He watched Poseidon abandon the gathering in a huff, his face red, his nostrils flared, his trident ready to stir trouble and start a storm somewhere in the bowl of the Aegean. Zeus turned his attention to Athena, who was frowning as she watched her uncle's departure. "Better track the winds picking up south of Crete," he said to her.

"I am, Father," answered Athena. "The winds are whipping along the shores. The coast is clear for Odysseus to return to Aeaea."

He smiled at his wise daughter.

Circe stood alone on the hillside, considering whether to meet with Glaucus one last time. She could see the fallacies in his obsession and knew that they mirrored her own—but she was ready to abandon the pursuit of her own fantasy. The residue inside her was relief and some sadness for the wasted effort, but the journey had been a good way to reset her own compass anew. He certainly would not miss her. She dismissed the thought and bent over the ground to collect some large, compact clusters of yellow yarrow, which stops bleeding and heals wounds of soldiers and gods alike. Odysseus could use some on his journey for the incidental scratches and wounds of the crew. She stepped deeper into the forest, away from the setting sun, and in the distance saw a cave. It could make a pleasant shelter for the night.

It was a shallow cave, the ground flat and covered with moss; there were thick ferns shading its entrance. She entered, pushing fronds aside. In the dim light and in a far corner, an enormous pair of round eyes stared at her. It was a white owl. *The owl of Athena*, she thought, *a good sign*. The bird waited for Circe to settle down and make a soft bed of fronds, then it flew away into the night.

While she rested her eyes, her thoughts returned to Glaucus one last time. A sense of sadness for him sprang up in her heart. She spied on him, to see his chest heaving, private tears escaping his eyes seamlessly blending with the seawater. Beautiful Skylla, youthful Skylla, unreachable Skylla. In his desperation, he had even asked her for a love potion. If he could only open his heart, he would see that many lovely Nereids, beautiful brides to choose from, surrounded him. And as Hypnos, the god of sleep, was taking her to the land where there is no light cast from the sun or the moon, she wondered when she would hear from Poseidon.

Rousing before dawn, she was nudged awake by the gentle tintinnabulation of bells from a romping herd of lambs sheltering nearby. When she stepped outside, in the sparkling clear sky she spotted a golden eagle perched on a craggy cliff below his nest. He was finishing his meal, a rabbit he had caught in his talons earlier, his yellow crooked beak plunging deep into its flesh until it was gone. Then he spread his long wings wide and slipped into gliding along wide swaths, just under the cloud cover. What was he looking for? she wondered.

Zeus's emissary was surveying the island for Circe. The magnificent bird—muscular, brown body; golden nape; and lighter wings dappled with white feathers—rested his eyes on her at the entrance of the cave. He took a deep dive, landing on a boulder close to her, folded his wings, then spread them wide and called her twice in his high-pitched cry. It was his invitation for her to approach, but Circe expected a sign from Poseidon and did not know the language of birds. She watched the eagle and took her time braiding her hair.

The bird lifted off the ground and quickly returned, repeating the show of spreading his wings and crying once more in this elaborate and persistent ritual. This time Circe considered the messenger and approached, carrying her satchel filled with the precious herb collection. When he stepped to the ground and lowered his body, she climbed onto his back. He was the answer to her request. Building momentum for his takeoff, he walked a few steps, ran, and then bounded with both feet, flapping his wings. She held on to his nape, and in an instant, she felt the lift, his powerful swing up to the sky.

EIGHTEEN

O nce airborne, they soared and glided, taking advantage of winds and thermals above the earth. At first, Zeus's eagle traveled high above the sea. His nape feathers fluttered in the wind, and Circe held on gently, resting her head on his soft plumage, glad that she had braided her hair that often lifted off her shoulders. They bonded their bodies to each other for the long day's journey; she felt every shift of his wings and each change in direction as he rode wind currents and responded to sky drafts.

From time to time, she leaned to view the blue watery surface below, interrupted by rocks, islands, swaths of earth, and dots of ships crossing the Mediterranean. Her lips recited spells she fashioned to coax fair winds for the journey, mantras that echoed in the ether. Meeting seagulls in flight, she would sing out to the divine master of winds, "I summon your sacred wings to carry us along, peaceful Aeolus." When strong thermals moved them along, she would urge, "Mighty winds, chart our way back home swiftly."

The eagle tore the skies, flapping his powerful outstretched wings, with tip feathers spread and separated in a show of royal majesty. She looked around in wonder, her eyes sparkling. It had to be Zeus's messenger. She muttered grateful praises to the father of all.

For a few minutes, her vision was blurry inside the gray mass of a cloud. Droplets of condensation formed on her body, giving her chills. Her father, Helios, was waiting to wrap her in his welcome radiant comfort as she cupped her eyes to protect them from the glare. She knew well that blurry state of mind. As she came out of it, the sun felt so steadying, so clarifying.

The eagle stayed in flight in a steadfast trajectory. By noon they were over the mainland. By dusk she sensed he was flying over the sea in lower altitudes. She could see surface currents following the whims of the wind and changing directions. She marveled at the beautiful earth below, with all humanity asleep and awake, doing and undoing. She loved them all, their struggles, their victories, their foils. Her days in Delos had awakened in her the awareness of sharing in their passions, and the beauty of their spirit. There was no place for the arrogance and disdain of Perse for mortals. Although she would never admit it, she loved them all, even this god, the heartbroken Glaucus. As the sun dipped behind the horizon line, Aeaea came into view, appearing so tiny, and her anticipation grew.

Zeus's eagle surveyed the landscape and landed on the ground at the grove next to her palace. Elated, Circe climbed down onto terra firma, stretched her limbs, and extended her hands to the eagle in a gesture of appreciation. Her delicate lips were chapped from the sun and the winds, and her throat was dry. She clapped her hands to get her servants' attention and walked to the crystal waters of a spring, filled her cupped hand, drank deeply, and then splashed water on her face. The eagle watched her from his perch on the branch of a tree. When she was done, she motioned him to the spring and thanked him with a slight bow. She searched for a better way to show her gratitude, but she did not know the language of birds. Turning toward her palace, she clapped her hands again to get the attention of her household. Where were her servants?

The eagle drank and fluffed his wings, bathing and oiling his feathers for a long minute. Circe bowed to him again, sensing his departure was imminent. He took a few steps, ran, and lifted off the ground with a final high-pitched goodbye.

A pair of silvery mountain wolves came out from the tall grasses at the edge of the grove, wagging their fluffy tails, and howled their welcome. She answered, howling right back, a greeting that returned a resounding echo to her ears. She applied salve to her lips and took the path leading to the silent pillars and the grand staircase. Lumbering up the stairs, she clapped her hands one more time. A faint song was coming from the great hall, voices of women harmonizing with an aulos, and as she closed in, she heard them vocalizing about the heroic deeds of the Greeks in Troy. They were singing rhapsodies about kings and warriors, about Hector, Paris, and the theft of enchanting Queen Helen. A small gathering of men enjoyed a meal in a room Circe had never allowed her maids to use. Shocked and cross, her ego bruised for she had expected a welcome, she advanced in fury. Elpinikis was the first to see her. He was about to greet her. "Mistress . . ."

She met his eyes, firing back lightning bolts. "In my absence . . ." Then she raised her wand, carved out of wood in the shape of a serpent, looked around, and cast a spell upon the room. In an instant, all turned into frozen columns, their bodies iced still. An angry grin deepened on her lips. "Fools! This will teach you!"

And there was Elpinikis, his eyes wide open, reaching out with a goblet of wine in his right hand. She seized his arm, and restored him, though his limbs remained stiff from the chill. He looked around the room and then at her in terror. Her might was undeniable. Circe had intended to give them a fright, to shake them like leaves. Most of all, she had to reinstate her authority.

"Witness the power of Circe, Elpinikis," she hissed and raged. "My house is not an entertainment center. Send your men away. I don't care how you do it. I want peace. As for you, I will deal with you soon." He winced and drew back, even though he had been among the warriors that fought next to Odysseus, Achilles, and Ajax, kings and heroes who had performed glorious deeds, just as he had done in battles in their service. Then, turning her back to them, Circe lifted her wand once more, murmured another spell, and cast her eyes on each person in the great hall. She watched their limbs thaw, coming to life. As they did, their eyes swept over the room, stopping on hers.

"Leave," Elpinikis commanded, urging the men toward the doors. One by one they fled the room hurriedly, cowered by the unexpected turn of events.

Moments later, Melis came running to see what the rumble of feet was about. She bowed and scraped to welcome her mistress. "Goddess," she whispered, kneeling at her feet, "welcome back."

"My house is not here to entertain slaves and servants," Circe asserted, "especially in my absence. Melis, how could you let this happen?"

Her servant's voice was measured, her eyes downcast when she spoke. "They worked so hard, sorting and carrying supplies to the cave for Odysseus, that I did not have the heart to stop them, my goddess. Elpinikis and his crew will soon face the cruel temper of Poseidon." She paused and looked at her mistress. "Tell me your wishes."

"Tonight I need to rest. Tomorrow I will praise and sacrifice to Zeus, who gave me passage back to Aeaea."

With that, Melis followed her along the hallways to her bedchamber and began preparing her bath. She started a fire in the hearth and set a pot of water to heat. "You will need some fresh clothes for the night, my mistress. You must be tired." She laid a gown on the bench.

"Yes. I just want to soak and rest my body tonight, Melis. Tell me what I missed while I was gone."

"The men worked hard. They respect Elpinikis and were pleased to load up food and blankets for the journey. At night, we heard stories about the battles in Troy, Achilles's bravery, and Odysseus's cunning. We heard about the Trojan horse they built and how they hid inside it. That's how they fooled the Trojans, who thought the Greeks were gone and let down their guard. That's how they captured Troy. They are rested and ready for the journey. They miss their home and women."

"And what of Elpinikis?"

Carefully holding the metal water jar by its handle with a folded cloth, Melis poured boiling water into the tub, mixed in some cold from a ceramic pot, stirred and tested it.

"He is a handsome man, if you ask me, and loyal to Odysseus." After fluffing up her mistress's bedding, she helped her untangle her hair, then waited as Circe finished combing. Although Melis had never shown an intrusive nature, she could not hold back a question. "And what of Glaucus, my mistress?"

Circe sighed, thinking, *Another misadventure*, and looked away. "A fantasy, already fading fast. Maybe someday I will tell you more." She tested her bathwater, added aromatic salts, removed her himation and tunic, and stepped into the steamy tub.

Melis watched her and smiled when she saw her mistress relax.

Soaking in the water, Circe felt the tightness in her body ease. She shut her eyes. What a day this had been: waking up in the cave, the eagle's plumage, their long flight, the great hall. She had been on overload and needed to let go. Melis was standing by, but all Circe wanted was to be alone, empty her mind. "Leave me, Melis," she said. "I am tired, out of sorts, and need my rest."

PART II

"When Circe saw me sitting there without eating, and in great grief, she came to me and said, 'Ulysses, why do you sit like that as though you were dumb, gnawing at your own heart, and refusing both meat and drink? Is it that you are still suspicious? You ought not to be, for I have already sworn solemnly that I will not hurt you.'

"And I said, 'Circe, no man with any sense of what is right can think of either eating or drinking in your house until you have set his friends free and let him see them. If you want me to eat and drink, you must free my men and bring them to me that I may see them with my own eyes.'"

—Homer, *The Odyssey*: Book 10.422–8
[*The Odyssey* (Trans. Samuel Butler)]

NINETEEN

onotony and boredom had settled over Aeaea after Odysseus's departure. Circe spent long stretches of her day laboring over her loom on new tapestries, using new materials to create unique designs. Her spinners turned out fine yarn and thread from the enchantress's herds of sheep and goats. She favored her skilled veterans who gathered to work outside the kitchen after the morning chores. With know-how, their nimble fingers turned out a rich array of choices for their mistress. On warm weather days, they moved to the shade, settling on benches under the eaves to gab and work during the lull in the day. Melis came before dinner and gathered the finished natural and dyed spools of thread they had dropped into a basket.

The girls wound animal and plant fibers onto spindles, twisting lengths of thread and wrapping them around the shafts. They moved like an orchestra in continuous motion, delivering fine-tuned results. Others worked on washing and dyeing using nature's palette: avocado pits for russet and pink, marigolds for yellow, hibiscus for pink, onion skins for soft caramel. Circe loved to watch them spin thread, pull on wee bits of yarn, twirl, pull, and wrap as they gossiped and took time to make clothes for themselves with spare thread. She often selected spools from the basket, asking for special favors, and sometimes joining their chatter.

The big news after Circe's return was that one of her spinners was expecting a baby, fathered by Elpinikis, who was on his way to Ithaca. Circe noticed her rounder belly. Although the young girl complained of nausea, nothing could dampen her joy about the baby. The envy of her friends, she would rub her belly with pride. Her best friend angled to share in the joys of motherhood and spoiled her, taking over her kitchen chores. Others made clothes for the baby and promised to give her relief when it was born. They hoped it would be a boy.

"I'll make you a drink that helps nausea. I'll give a bottle to Melis for you," Circe offered.

As she rose to take her leave, a servant asked, "Any news from Odysseus? Are he and his men safe and back in Ithaca?"

Circe paused. She believed that Odysseus's loyalty to his wife and his yearning for home had stolen him from her, but she also wondered if this was love for Penelope or his possessive nature for what he claimed to be his. Finally, she answered the servant, "Tiresias warned him about more future hardships. I coached him on how to survive sailing past the island of the Sirens, and he wisely followed my guidance."

Retiring to her darkened bedroom, she looked into her scrying mirror, with which Circe tracked life beyond the island on the hour after the evening meal. Etched in obsidian and silver, the mirror was a gift from Hecate, the pale goddess of boundaries, crossroads, and divination. Its silver back depicted the mysterious goddess gazing at the moon.

This night, she was eager to know how Odysseus had fared with the Sirens, who were well known for enticing sailors to their destruction with their irresistible singing. Usually, sailors were so completely absorbed by the ethereal voices that they wrecked their ships and drowned. Now she saw how it had gone: When his ship approached their island, Odysseus ordered his men to plug their ears with beeswax and tie him to the mast.

He wanted the experience of hearing their songs, even though he knew the danger. When their divine voices tempted him, he begged his men to release him from his fetter, but they followed his instructions and did not, and the ship sailed on to Ithaca.

Despite herself, she smiled. *How like him to tempt the Sirens,* she thought.

Her scrying mirror also helped Circe keep up with her parents. They were often looking for recognition and enduring glory, forming new alliances, and building prestige. Her father loved any attention to the life-giving sun in songs, pictures, and objects. In his palace, he had assembled sun-themed frescoes, sculptures, rugs—he even had the eating utensils etched with sunbursts. At gatherings, musicians and vocalists praised Helios's life force and splendor. He was Circe's sun, a father she adored when she was young. Growing up, she came to recognize that he was an essential part of spring and the revival of life.

In recent days, the sorceress had woven a tapestry for him, a crown of sunlight that penetrated lavish spring fields strewn with wildflowers. Unique blends of yellows and greens dotted the tapestry next to gentle, pale petals and vibrant reds and purples. She added fine and coarse ribbons and threads that came to life when breezes rustled them into a gentle dance. When she completed the design, she removed it from the loom, finishing it with a fringe of golden threads along the edge. Melis gasped when she saw it complete. "My mistress, only a goddess could weave so much glory and light into a tapestry!"

Before calling on her father to present him with her gift, she checked her obsidian mirror to find her parents in the midst of another argument, on the verge of separation. Perse's latest demand was that Helios build her a separate wing in his palace with a splendid hall all her own and a view of Mount Olympus.

She had invited old Cybele, the Great Mother of the Gods—gray hair, sagging breasts—and Perse needed a court suitable to receive the revered old-timer. Helios viewed this as one of her greedier and more unnecessary ultimatums, as Cybele had not even accepted the invitation. He considered Perse's quarters not only adequate but ostentatious.

The argument had ended with him sending her away from his bed. It had been going on for a week, during which angry Perse roamed the Mediterranean sending him daily messengers with designs for the remodel. Circe had seen her mother's endless hunger for more of everything in times past. *Father is fed up*, she thought. Watching her parents, she often thought that they would be better off leading separate lives.

In the dawn's early light, she met him wearing her silk tunic painted with spring wildflowers and a himation made of sheer, pale green tulle, gathered at her shoulders and held with a pair of elegant sun clasps, a gift from him. When Helios received his daughter's present, he ran his hand across its surface, sensing the motion she had woven into this still-life tapestry, fueled by the sun's rays and energy. "Daughter, your artistry is amazing! I will have it hanging in my great hall, where visitors can admire it. You shine with unusual talents; none of this is wasted on your father or those Olympians who favor you."

Circe glowed that morning, pleased with her father's appreciation. She spoke softly, tilting her head coyly, "Proud to be your daughter," and watched his chariot move on to bring light to the waking world.

Then she took the path to her herb hut, moving through the woods, gathering chamomile flowers along the way to replenish her supply. Melis could brew a hot drink for her pregnant spinner who carried Elpinikis's child. Circe meant to remind her that the scent of lemon mixed with honey in hot water should help overcome nausea. As she leaned down to gather flowers, a couple of forest rabbits scurried away to find their food in a safer spot. She smiled to herself, content to be on her island, surrounded by her herbs, her animals, and her people.

Around the turn in her path, in the shadow of a pine tree, she found herself pinned by the gaze of an unpleasant visitor. She took a deep breath, recognizing Perse, and before she could greet her, her mother spoke accusingly. "When a daughter forgets her mother . . . who gave her life . . . she deserves little happiness," she fumed.

Circe bristled at the sudden attack. "Mother, what is this all about? What did I do this time?"

"You are inconsiderate, no different from that monster that eats sailors. Someday you will be sorry you are neglecting your mother. You never give *me* presents."

The hint was transparent. Her mother never hesitated to ask for what she wanted, but the comment about a monster eating sailors made no sense. Circe tossed her hair back and furrowed her brow. She had had enough of her mother's hints and name-calling. No longer a child, Circe had some advice to give her. Gathering her courage, she responded, "You want something, but you don't know how to ask when you call me a monster."

Perse paced back and forth, muttering just loud enough to be heard: "Just like her father! How dare she! Both of them turning a deaf ear to me." She stopped pacing, squared her shoulders, and declared, "Your father is building me a new wing suitable for housing my people and receiving my guests. I need one of your tapestries showing the magic gardens Glaucus took you to."

Circe answered, feeling heat on her cheeks, "There is no new wing to fill; Helios will not build you one. As for Glaucus, that is all behind me. He is sorting out his life with Skylla, and I don't want to rekindle those memories."

An angry Perse raised her voice and, before disappearing, tossed a last spiteful remark, "Sorting? You better go back to your scrying mirror and see what a mess he is in. You are a thankless daughter. I have had enough of you today!"

TWENTY

*A*fter Perse's sudden departure, Circe continued gathering chamomile flowers that smiled out of the soil. She found them at the usual sunny spot year after year and collected them in a handy goatskin pouch. Once she had enough for her spinner and her servants, a large pile, she took the dappled path to the herb hut.

Her mother stayed on her mind. Perse was a smart, ambitious woman, but needy and greedy—and deeply troubled. Sometimes Circe thought their connection had broken like thin glass into a thousand shards and was beyond rebuilding. Perhaps her mother's demanding nature and constant call for attention came from being one of the three thousand daughters of the Titans Oceanus and Tethys. One of three thousand daughters . . . yet she was not lost in that number. She had won the attention of Helios, who had several wives and consorts. With her charm and beauty, she stood out and pursued him until he took her as one of his wives. But this meant only more competition. Standing out for Perse must have meant survival. Anyway, Circe was glad she had stood up to her and exposed the lie. She knew her annoyed father would never build a new wing for her mother.

Still, the encounter with Perse had darkened Circe's mood, spoiling her warm exchange with Helios, the pleasure she had felt in his response to her gift, and her own satisfaction with her work. Enough! She would treat herself to a day of roaming and pastimes she enjoyed.

At once the sky darkened with a flock of thousands of starlings. Gathered in a cloud, the shivering mass moved along to form a new pattern of intersecting bubbles, as if someone had given a command. The cloud metamorphosed again into a sphere, its thickness shifting to the center, persistent and eerie. Circe watched them vanish into the west, but they soon reappeared, beating their wings frantically.

The cause was soon clear: a falcon. His hungry wanderlust had led him to the flock, which immediately changed direction, making a rapid turn for a better chance of surviving the ruthless predator. The mob of starlings that were spared the falcon's talons fluttered their wings and rushed away, beyond the horizon line. All was quiet, and Circe threaded her fingers through her hair. Was it an omen?

Arriving at the door to her hut, she moved to the counter and eagerly reached to the lower shelf for the abalone shell box Glaucus had given her. She inspected the precious prickly herb of eternal youth that floated inside it. She had kept it in salt water. It was vibrant and thorny, very much alive, oozing a little milky white cloud, possibly because she had moved it. Memories of Delos flooded in: the formidable rock, the fishmonger, the amphibian, and Skylla. She remembered the wounded look in Glaucus's eyes each time the young girl ignored him. What kind of trouble could he be in?

She wrote a couple of notes, including a reminder about keeping the herb in salt water, and formed a hypothesis connecting motion to the clouding she had noticed. She also noted where Glaucus described that he found it, and then returned the abalone shell box to the shelf. There was more to record later. Maybe tonight she would have time to look into her mirror to learn about Glaucus's predicament. For now, she wanted to catalog his gift and begin studying it in the weeks that followed.

Circe kept old dusty notes about each herb in her possession, capturing observations and possible combinations in her neat handwriting. She stacked them in a cubby above the shelves, and they contained her entries from years of foraging and learning. She used them to record ways of healing people and animals, for a better life and death. A meticulous record keeper, she studied and logged new insights. Some pages held secret recipes Hecate had given her, but most were Circe's own notes. She listed the properties of each substance, including what part of the plant was useful (leaves, roots, or flowers) and in what form (whole, pulverized, boiled). There were notes about frequency and amounts to use, impact, and effective ways to combine with other plants.

She thought about her pregnant spinner's needs, what would be useful during her pregnancy, childbirth, and for the care of the baby. A new life would be a blessing on Aeaea. Circe sighed, for she had not birthed a child yet knew how precious and short life is for mortals. Although this baby was not her own, the thought of new life stirred in her warm, maternal instincts. She would take good care of this mom and child.

Circe gathered a few jars and pouches to keep handy at the house. Her chamomile pile needed more attention. Her servants would pick the flowers off the stems and dry them in the sun. The girls made tea and used it both to reduce inflammation and swelling and to encourage relaxation. Her pregnant spinner would have it to help with her nausea. Echinacea was handy for overcoming colds and flu. She added a jar of feverfew leaves for Melis, who used them to treat her migraines, and started for the house.

It was getting late for dinner, and she needed sustenance. Up ahead, she saw the shady arbor, heavy with purple clusters of grapes she could not resist. She reached for a clump. A lover of fruit, she had planted several varieties on her island and liked them fresh or dried. Sweet grapes exploded with aromatic flavors in her mouth, and she ate every last grape, spitting out the seeds as she trudged along the rest of the way home.

Only Melis had seen Circe's good nature. She often said to the others, "Our mistress is not just an artful weaver and master of herbs. She is a powerful healer, not the dark sorceress some fear."

Now she waited in the quiet house for her mistress to return. Even the kitchen had grown quiet, though savory food smells still wafted in the air. The cooks were the last to eat, and a few were still finishing their meal. Most everyone had retired. Then the enchantress arrived, and Melis noticed dark circles had formed under Circe's eyes.

"Hello, Melis. I brought some herbs for the house." Circe rested her load on a table, took a few chamomile plants out of the pouch, and showed Melis how to separate the flowers and toss the rest. Her movements were slow and precise. She instructed, "Place the flowers in trays and set them in the shade to dry." Then she handed her a jar. "Here, for your migraines."

Melis, who knew the routine, saw how tired and dispirited Circe seemed tonight. She waited for her to finish, then offered, "I have food prepared for you, or maybe you prefer a drink. It will not take long to serve you. Shall I?" She collected all the jars and the pouch with chamomile as she waited to hear her mistress's wishes.

Circe drew a deep breath and started for the house. "No, not tonight. It's been a long day. I will see you in the morning. Goodnight."

In her bedroom, when she thought of Glaucus, Circe felt an old pain of disappointment rising in her chest. Still, she had wonderful memories from Delos: the port, the temples, the fish-monger. She had not heard from Skylla at all. *She must be fine,* the enchantress concluded.

Circe picked up her scrying mirror and sat on her bench, her mother's words ringing in her ears. "What mess could Glau-cus be in?" she mumbled to herself. Holding the mirror firmly, she repeated his name, focusing her mind, and peered deeply into the smooth obsidian. She waited for the cloudy surface to clear and form a picture. Nothing.

She paused, rubbed her eyes in frustration, called his name louder, and looked again. All she could see was undefined smoke, the kind that emanates from a chimney toward the dark evening sky. No Glaucus. *Is he all right? Is he in distress?*

Too tired to persist, she decided that everything was proba-bly just fine. She might try again tomorrow.

TWENTY-ONE

The next morning found Circe at her spinner house, freshly stocked with supplies. Bent over her loom, she removed a length of cloth she intended for the unborn baby. The new project would be for herself. Circe loved elegant, long pieces of cloth to drape over her body for auspicious appearances. A new fabric for the autumn is what she needed.

Her young brother used to tell her she looked best in the pale palette of spring, but today she was drawn to the strong primary colors of summer. Odysseus preferred those. She laid some spools on the floor to settle on a color scheme: reds, blues, and yellows of different thicknesses. She imagined creating colorful swirls on a neutral background, a design sure to stand out anywhere she went.

Taking a few steps back, the goddess considered her first selections. No, no . . . The colors were too strong. Together, they might clash. Perhaps the softer cyan, a paler magenta and yellow. Cloth woven with finer thread would be best for a flowing effect. Placing new spools on her chest, she tested different combinations in a mirror. Finally, she sat at her loom to prepare it and begin using the softer colors.

Circe labored over three hours to create two stretched palms of length, but nothing was going smoothly. She ran her hands over the length, touching the cloth lightly. It was the yellow thread, knotty and thicker than her magenta and cyan yarn. It bulged out and ruined the effect she desired to have: a smooth, even, draping cloth. By midday, frustrated, she thought of starting over. There was no magic to her artistry today. The threads rebelled, and she could not settle on an approach. She was getting impatient.

She was frowning when Melis, perhaps having heard the disruption in the rhythmic sound of the shuttle, walked in to tidy up the room. For a moment, both were silent, and then the servant spoke. "It would be easier for me to tidy up if I could have the room to myself," she said, looking directly at Circe and then at the floor, where spools were strewn around haphazardly.

The enchantress sprang to her feet. "I have had enough for today anyway." She tossed her words into the air and breezed past Melis, deserting the room. Relieved to abandon her project, Circe descended down a path she had not taken in a long time. It was a green strip of land that led to the beach. Out of sorts, she moved down close to the coastline.

It was a muggy day; the air was thick with humidity. Her hair felt dry and unmanageable. Glad that there was no one around to notice, Circe recognized the shore where dolphins had picked her up before her journey to Delos. The sea always soothed her. Seagulls were gliding by the shore, looking for their daily meal. She sat on a log the tide had drifted onto the sandy shore, smooth, stripped of its bark. *I should come down here more often,* she thought. It was her heritage, after all; she was the daughter of a Nereid. The heat and the sultriness felt unseasonably high, more like middle of the summer than late fall.

The sky grew darker as her father, Helios, abandoned Aeaea, turning his reign over to clouds and the swirly winds of Aeolus. In the distance, the sorceress heard a roar and sensed a disturbance. In deeper waters, a twister lifted up the sea to the sky in a dark funnel. The waterspout built up speed and pushed its way to the shore, releasing heavy drops over land and sea. It was unusual to have the elements force their way over Aeaea. The goddess was excited, taking in the force and might of the thunderstorm. The power and mood suited her today. She danced and watched the waterspout switch back and forth, not minding it when the downpour washed her face, dress, and shoes. Just as suddenly as it appeared, the thunderstorm dissipated, after unloading kelp on the shore and marking the hillside with tiny brooks.

Thinking of Glaucus and the algae he had shown her that healed the wounds of the man caught in a hunting accident, she gathered some kelp to dry and study later on. The thrill of watching nature's power was over soon, as the twister weakened and moved away. Circe shivered, cold and drenched, and rushed home.

That night, back in her room, the enchantress lay on her bed, shut her eyes to release the tension stored in her limbs, and tuned in to her contemplative mind. She emptied the chatter and quieted her thoughts to find herself in a dreamy state, one filled with images. The stage of her mind was filled with her beloved mountain lions that usually hovered around the palace. They came into sharp focus: a lion mother with her cubs and the gray wolves, moving in slow motion. They aged quickly in front of her eyes, only to fade into the clouds.

Circe did not follow them. Notions of birth and death, the distillation of her experiences seized her mind. In nature she had seen thousands of beginnings and as many endings. Although immortal, she carried the weight, the grieving of loss, and many memories. So did Aeetes, her brother. They had been raised under her parents' protection, but like most teens, they hungered for independence. She had willingly left the palace a week after her brother took his leave. He moved to rule Colchis, a kingdom on the eastern edge of the Black Sea. Circe missed him. In her dream this night, he appeared as a young, blond teen practicing fencing. She wished they had stayed in touch, but—absorbed with the responsibilities of their domains—they had drifted apart.

As she was falling asleep, Glaucus's face slipped in. Although Hypnos was sitting heavy on her eyelids, the thought of Glaucus forced her eyes open and she got up. Uneasy and determined, she picked up a shawl, draped it over her shoulder, and checked around the bedroom. She felt the urge to consult her scrying mirror at once.

TWENTY-TWO

*C*irce doused her obsidian mirror in cleansing water and dried it with a white, absorbent cloth. Back in her bed, she leaned into some pillows and whispered praises to Hecate, asking for her help. The full moon was out tonight, ensuring that Circe's powers were heightened. Focusing her energy to the center of the mirror, she called his name: "Glaucus . . ."

The obsidian clouds parted swiftly, revealed the blue waters of Poseidon's kingdom. Circe discerned an amphibian figure, sitting by a coral reef alone, bent over barren sand. There was no sign of Nereids, no garden, only hard coral piled high behind him and shadows that swayed around him. She wanted to read his face. Why did he stay doubled down, moaning incomprehensible laments?

The shadowy spirits pressed on him. Their ghostly presence emanated groans and dread. A pitiful chorus. Circe held her breath and called out, "Glaucus . . ." although she knew he could not hear her. It had to be Glaucus, but his slick fish body was not shimmering in the sea, not even his beautiful tail. Strangely covered by a mass of floating kelp, Glaucus blended with the dark spirits.

The shadows that circled him stopped mumbling and swaying, and suddenly awake, they started a frantic song, their formless hands reaching for his flesh and shrieking, "Vengeful monster . . . sad imposter . . . you are guilty ever after . . . no more laughter."

So he *was* being punished—but for what?

Bounding upward, he shook his arms unexpectedly through the air, his eyes dull and pained. He turned toward the sky and cried, "Skylla, will you ever forgive me?" Then he folded in two, dropping into his sea of sorrow.

"Never . . . never . . . never . . ." answered the Furies.

Just as unexpectedly, Circe was overcome with a wave of sadness. The image of the sea world had turned dark and bitter. The dreamy land of the Nereids, the garden, Poseidon's rituals were all absent, and Glaucus's world spelled loneliness and pain. The Furies had poisoned the sea with a sense of decay that made her shudder. "Glaucus," she called again, although he could not hear her. "What have you done?"

As though her words had cut through the veil of muck, those images vanished, and a familiar face came on the scrying mirror's surface. It was her mother, Perse, in person, with her perfectly applied lipstick and rouge, perfumed and fanning herself arrogantly. She only uttered, "No poisons! I told you so," and faded away!

Yes, Circe remembered the warning to keep knowledge about dangerous herbs away from Glaucus, advice that she had ignored. Her unpredictable mother had tried to warn her. But hadn't Perse encouraged her to seek a doomed relationship with Glaucus the day she was foraging for herbs in Delos? Had she known about Skylla then? The enchantress concluded that Perse had come only to add to her daughter's discomfort, to remind her she had been right.

Circe got up and began to pace. She pulled the drapes open for fresh air and looked outside. The sky was pinned with bright, pale stars, but no reassurance. Something horrible, beyond what she could imagine, had unfolded in Delos. Something had happened to Skylla—something so unforgivable that the gods were punishing Glaucus, torturing him with Furies spitting pangs of guilt. "Sad imposter," they hissed. "Vengeful monster."

Even worse, though, was the silence. The air was still; Skylla had not called for her help. A sordid parade ran through Circe's mind: hurt, pain, wound, murder, swords, knives, herbs, and poisons. What weapon did he use? Did he hurt Skylla? Could it be someone else? What had he done?

She walked outside the house to calm her nerves. Hecate's moon was smiling in its mysterious pale way, giving her no answers. Only her mirror could reveal what had happened. She would have to look for Skylla.

Where had her mirror gone? Had she, in her confusion, taken it from her bedroom? Had she brought it along outside and dropped it? Backtracking, she searched the path, returned to the staircase, climbed up the stone steps, and was back in her bedroom. No mirror anywhere. In the silence of the night, she heard the call of an owl in the distance. It was coming from the northwest. Was it Athena, who had been Odysseus's protector during the Trojan War and on his journey home? About now, Odysseus and his crew must be past the Sirens, heading for the Strait of Messina.

Especially tonight, Circe hated the dark. She called Melis, ordered her to light torches, and retraced her steps. The owl hooted again from somewhere near the staircase. It was hard to concentrate; her thoughts were in disarray, but still she knew that an eagle, a falcon, and now an owl were all emissaries of the Olympians. Nature had entered into her life in significant ways. She herself had shifted briefly into a sandpiper. Birds witnessed life from above. What was the message?

But where was her mirror? She fled the bedroom, so upset that she had lost track of it. Pressing on her temples, she concentrated, demanding a sign. A lame glow was coming from near the newel post of her staircase. She ran up the steps and saw the scrying mirror on the landing. It was not broken.

Back in her bedroom, the mirror in her hands, she sat and focused, calling Skylla's name. The obsidian surface cleared, revealing a ghastly sight, a mass perched by a rock, thrusting around. Were those tentacles? Was that a mouth? More? It surely was not Skylla!

Searching for what had gone wrong, Circe worried she had not paid proper tribute to Hecate tonight and the image was false. The scrying mirror had worked when she sought out Glaucus. She checked the room. The drapes were still drawn. It was dark, and no one was around except for an owl. Perched on the capital of a column, the bird had fixed yellow, round eyes on her, like a mystical messenger from Athena. Circe held the mirror tenuously, still staring at that elegant black surface, etched with Hecate's image, and called for her help.

"Skylla," she uttered again.

This time a clear image of the Strait of Messina appeared. It was that narrow channel where Charybdis, the mighty whirlpool, waited to swallow ships and sailors in her swirl. Had Odysseus gone through it yet? He was a skillful navigator; she had warned him and had faith in his skills, still . . . But where was Skylla?

Across from Charybdis, the seeing mirror returned the full view of a grotesque monster. It had to be the same one she had seen minutes ago. With a closer look, she counted twelve feet and six dog heads lined up, each with a triple row of sharp teeth. The creature was perched by a rock opposite Charybdis. The new enemy threatened Odysseus, and all who would try to cross the strait. *So many mouths sprouting from this body! This is not human, too grotesque to be considered an animal*, thought Circe. The owl called, and the goddess instinctively checked the other side of the strait.

Odysseus had made it through! His face was washed in sea salt, his black hair was matted, and he held on to the mast, shouting at his men to row faster. What a relief! The ship sailed toward the opposite end of the strait. Circe surveyed the ship, counting his men; six were missing.

When the monster burped, limbs escaped from her mouth, human limbs. The cannibal had devoured his men, and the waters swallowed them up. Six warriors from Troy were gone unsung, their dreams of home crushed on the bloody rocks of the Strait of Messina.

Then Circe heard a bark—and two more followed. Another sorry yelp. Altogether six. They were coming from the monster. Six barking dogs. DOGS!

Skylla, the monster dog? Was this the young girl Glaucus loved, transformed into a dog? Leaping to her feet, Circe screened every inch of the three kilometers through the strait, carefully scanning every rock, searching again for Odysseus.

In the calm waters of the Ionian Sea, out of the strait, a bare vessel sailed with a ragged man steadying himself against the sway of the boat and all his sailors mourning. It was Odysseus, the son of Laertes, who had lost six sailors, among them Elpinikis, to the deadly monster, eight men who would never see sweet Ithaca.

TWENTY–THREE

Circe had been weaving since dawn, her mind running in a million directions, sending the shuttle across delicate threads. Those tiny, rhythmic throws helped her put some order to her thoughts. After all, in the beginning the universe was chaos. Despite their internal struggles and entanglements with mortals, gods had put some order in the world. She had done her part in Aeaea. The mirror's revelations had left her in a bewildered state, yet she knew things begin anew when one finds a starting point.

She abandoned the loom and breathed a deep sigh of relief, glad to have seen Odysseus alive, although alone and disheveled. He had survived, her advice had paid off, and Tiresias had helped. There were many hardships to face before reaching Ithaca, and he had been cautious. She moved to the window, pushed the curtains aside, and looked outside, listening to birds trilling their songs. She did not need to feel stress about him. That made it easy to decide. She would return to Delos.

Melis came into the weaving room for the daily tidying up and stopped inside the doorway to admire Circe's nearly finished baby blanket. She had used pastel-green thread for the background and decorated it using marigold-yellow yarn for the sunbursts, gray puffs of fiber for the clouds, and multiple colors for the birds.

Melis carried the basket loaded with spools to her mistress. "Soft and pretty! It will keep the baby warm in the winter months." Stroking the spools, she selected and handed a couple to the goddess. "Here are some ivory threads for the edging."

Circe examined them for softness and strength and raised one to her cheek. "Well done. Another couple of months and we will have a baby on Aeaea," she said, tying knots on the surface of the blanket to secure loose threads. "I will finish it in two days before I leave."

"She is very pregnant and carries the baby high in her belly. It's probably a boy." There was delight in the old woman's voice.

"Sit down, Melis. We have some planning to do. I am leaving for Delos."

"Delos again, mistress?" Her voice registered surprise, her eyebrows raised.

"My friends on the island need my help. But before I leave, tell me, are we ready for the winter?"

"The cellars are full. We are prepared," answered Melis, who had many questions, but Circe's tone did not allow inquiries. "How long will you be away?"

"Hard to know. Maybe a week. I will leave in three days. Let me know if you need me to take care of anything."

Although Circe knew that Elpinikis and another five sailors of Odysseus's crew had not survived the Strait of Messina and were on their way to Hades, she decided to keep this from her people until after the baby was born and after she had learned more in Delos.

In the early hours of the third day, she was at the promontory, preparing to lift off. Larger than ten of the biggest eagles put together, she grew black feathers on her body and white feathers on her belly and fanned her tail. Her yellow eagle eyes surveyed the horizon. She spread out and flapped her wide wings, and was airborne, easily riding the airwaves that lifted her up to a sky view of the coastline. To get used to her new form, she rode the currents, staying over Aeaea. She loved her island. The land was resting after the summer harvests, green and brown, adorned by the calm sea. Circe set her course for Delos. Yesterday's sacrifice and prayers to Aeolus, the god of winds, had been answered. His light breath lifted her on a smooth, direct route to her destination.

Although she had traveled this route before, in the company of dolphins and riding on an eagle, this was an ever-changing sight, a surreal experience. She loved the lift, the flow, the ease of it, and did not mind it when her wings and tail feathers felt droplets form as she moved through a heavy-laden cloud. It covered her with fresh, cooling water that soon dried in the sun. The breeze felt good on her face. She grew comfortable navigating in the vast expanse around her.

The changing autumn weather marked acres of frothing waters below. This time of the year, the sea was dangerous, the winds strong, and many seafaring sailors had returned home. Fewer galleys were crossing the Mediterranean, and the last flocks of birds rushed by to reach warmer climates. For a while, she was flying next to a colony of seagulls that had lifted from an Aegean island, rushing for the African coast. She sped ahead, aiming to arrive at the silver island before sunset.

She reviewed the images she had seen in the mirror. Circe had some clues, but she was unclear about what had transpired on Delos during these past six months. What had happened to Skylla? Why had the girl not called her? Was she the monster? What had Glaucus done?

By sunset, her destination was visible. A swirl of emotions overtook her when she saw the port and the Propylaea on the hill. Her excitement to return to the recent adventure site was mixed with worry about what she might find. She aimed for the port. Many boats had been pulled to dry dock for the winter. Aristos had secured his, covering it with canvas, but the fish-monger was nowhere to be seen.

She landed on the hill behind the sanctuaries and moved behind the brush, shook her wings and tail off, shedding her feathers as a strong wind took them away. After shape-shift-ing into her former self, she started out for Poseidon's temple, where she would spend the night.

TWENTY-FOUR

The crowds on the hill were already sparse and the shops had closed, but Aristos's brother, the priest, was still in conversation with a young woman in the temple of Poseidon. Despite his attention to the devotee, he was aware when Circe entered the temple. He immediately recognized her. The woman, seeing Circe, thanked the priest and took her leave.

"Welcome back, goddess," said the priest; bowing in respect, he offered her the hospitality of the temple. As she approached him, he took in the impressive image: tall and gracious, in a light blue tunic and pleated dark blue himation, she wore sun-face silver earrings, a silver belt decorated with turquoise stones, and a matching tiara.

"My good man, I will spend the night here. But what I want is information. How is your brother? Have you any news about Glaucus and Skylla?"

Seeing that Circe was upset, the priest wrung his hands and answered cautiously, "My brother is fine. He would be glad to see you, but I have no news about the others. Neither has been seen, my goddess." Circe nodded, scowling. He realized she was aware they were missing. "Skylla's father went to the rock to plead for Glaucus's help, but the amphibian never showed up." He noticed Circe holding her wand tightly, her knuckles white.

"Who was the last one to see Skylla?"

"A boy from her village saw her going for her morning swim a week ago. He was the last one to see her." The priest gazed at her intently.

"I made a promise to myself to shield this young sister," said Circe. "Something has gone wrong. I am going to the rock tomorrow to find out what."

Leaving the sleeping temples at the crack of dawn, Circe walked down the hill, heading for the rock, musing about the scrying mirror's revelations that had brought her to Delos. She took the path to the sea where the rhythmic whispers of the waves delivered messages beyond her understanding. Poseidon's world held many secrets, and some were dark.

At Skylla's beach, she saw a young man curled up asleep under the pines. She recognized him: he was the boy who had hidden the girl's clothes some time ago. Circe approached the rock and sat on dry sand. Placing her hands around her lips, she formed a funnel and called out, "Glaucus . . ." Her voice bounced off the rock and returned with a "cus . . . cus . . . cus." Waiting expectantly, she repeated her call, but no one appeared. She stayed there trying to penetrate with her wand for any signs. There was no use.

When the young man awoke, he sat up and rubbed his eyes. Seeing Circe, he dusted off his clothes to shake off the sand. She approached him and gently asked, "Were you waiting for Skylla?" He nodded and cracked his knuckles, twisting the ring he wore on his pinky.

"I am here to help." The goddess moved next to him and petted his black, curly hair, as a mother would. "How long have you known her?"

"Since we were young," he answered wearily. "We are from the same village." It had been six months since the day Circe first met him. He had seemed like only a boy that day, when he came to the beach with his friend, hoping to talk with Skylla and hid her clothes. Six months is a long time for the young. Had Skylla shown preference for this lad? Now he did not pull away from Circe, nor did he look at her directly, a sign of respect for her position as the goddess from Aeaea.

"You must miss her. Tell me what you know." Already she knew he was living on scorched earth, afraid his girl was gone forever.

"She has not been back." His voice wavered anxiously. "It has been several days."

"What was she doing when you saw her last?"

"She was swimming. There was a swirl in the water. It sucked her away. I have not seen her since. But she is such a splendid swimmer . . . Maybe she took a dive, and she'll return."

"Did you see Glaucus?"

"He was in the distance but faded under the sea."

Still, the waves repeated his despair: "faded . . . faded . . . faded . . ." Her eyes softened. *Oh, the hopes and pain of young love.* "Go home. Wait for her at home, in the village. I will bring her back."

Lovelorn, the young man stared into the distance. "She may not want to come back. Who knows where she is? Temptations might keep her there."

Circe waved her arms in the air, as if dispelling clouds of doubt. "Is there a sweeter place than home? Remember that she loves you and has a strong, determined ally in me!"

His eyes brightened and a smile formed on his lips. "Will I see her again? Soon?"

"You will, my son; you will. Within the month."

With that assurance, he thanked her and took the path to the village.

Circe returned to the shore by the rock with a sinking feeling. Were her calls unheard or ignored? Still, she called again, using her hands to form a funnel, "Glaucus, Glaucus, I am here. Come to the rock."

She was getting ready to return to the temples when a slender swimmer answered her calls, nearing the rock from afar. Circe watched, wondering who the swimmer might be. It was a Nereid she had met when she followed Glaucus to Poseidon's underwater gardens. Pandora, daughter of Nereus, in her ivory tunic decorated with coral, climbed onto the rock and spoke to Circe. "Enchantress of Aeaea, he is not coming. He has been shunned by us who witnessed his vengeance. I come at the behest of Poseidon to tell you his punishment is to live alone. The Furies are his only company."

"What did he do, dear Pandora? Tell me. Did he hurt Skylla?"

"He had received an oracle that he would be tied to her forever. He loved her."

Circe nodded. "I know."

"When he realized she was pining for a mortal boy, his love turned to vengeance."

"What did he do, Pandora?"

"He thrust a vial of mushroom venom into the waters, killing sea creatures and turning her into a monster who lives at the Strait of Messina."

Circe bit her lip, remembering her gifts, his fascination with new herbs, but especially the mysterious mushrooms that held powers of good and evil. He must have studied them, tested the proportions in the sea, and then created the vile venom that transformed Skylla. Was it on purpose? Was it a mistake?

She shook her head and raised a fist into the air. He had abused his powers, striking this beautiful sister who had signaled for a long time her disinterest in him. Worse yet, he had used the mushrooms she had gifted him as his vengeful weapon. This was an outrage! Worse than she could have imagined.

Pandora bowed her head. "I was the closest to Glaucus and the most distressed by what occurred. I am relieved now to see that you also care about what he did."

"Tell me, Pandora."

"He meant to take her beauty away, certain that was what attracted her mortal suitors, hoping that this way he could keep her to himself. He had no regard for her wishes. But his concoction was too strong. She turned into a barking monster."

"That is desperate love, Pandora." Her voice reverberated in anger. "He's crossed boundaries."

"Once he told me that goats would have to walk on the ocean floor and fish would climb to the top of mountains before he stopped loving her. I was there all along to help him, but he could not see me," Pandora confessed, her words enfolded in a veil of grief.

"'Ερως ανίκατε μάχαν (Love, you who are unconquerable in battle)'—invincible even when you try to fight it," said Circe, quoting from Sophocles's *Antigone*. She had nearly been caught in its webs one more time. She thanked the Nereid profusely. "It clears my confusion, dear Pandora. I will be forever thankful to Poseidon and to you for sharing what you know. I want to help Skylla. As for Glaucus, he deserves his punishment."

"He is repenting, but it is too late. What lives in the hearts of men and gods is a mystery to me." Then Pandora continued, her voice urgent, "Restore her, Circe! That will be a relief to us all." With that, she faced the horizon line, dove into the water, and started on her journey back to the liquid kingdom.

The priest was securing the vestments for the night when he heard someone enter the shadows in the hushed interior of the temple. He saw it was Circe, and there was no mistaking the anger and exhaustion she bore. Hours earlier, the village boy had come to him, proclaiming that Skylla would return. News traveled fast on the island, and priests were a repository of both the trite and the important.

Now he rubbed his hands together in his concern for the girl. "Where is she, goddess? What happened to her?"

"She settled at the Strait of Messina," she said curtly, "but no need to spread rumors; I will fetch her and bring her back to her father soon."

"How did she get that far?" he pressed.

But Circe would not give him the sordid details. "The temple is more important to supplicants than ever before," she told him. "Glaucus is not returning to his rock anytime soon. As for me, I will be gone in the morning."

He would have insisted on more of an explanation, but she had turned away and was getting ready for her night's rest.

TWENTY-FIVE

*P*horkys, Skylla's father, a graying man who had lost his wife soon after his daughter's birth, worried about his child when she did not return home by midnight. He tossed and turned all night long, and the next morning, after feeding the chickens, he took to the streets. First, he followed the path she usually took for her daily swim and ran into a couple of peddlers. They were brothers that frequented the village selling necklaces, earrings, buckles, and other trinkets for the women. The one with a pronounced limp had laid his crutch on the ground and was shaking out the sand from his sandals. Phorkys greeted them and asked, "Have you seen my daughter, by any chance?"

"We saw her yesterday walking to the beach," the older brother answered. "Why? Is there something wrong?"

"She did not come home last night. It's not like her," Phorkys answered with a pained expression in his eyes.

"Probably out with her young fellow," the crippled boy chuckled as he picked up his crutch. Phorkys ignored his comment and, without a goodbye, continued on the path to the deserted beach to search for any sign of Skylla. As he was ready to give up, he saw one of her sandals under the pine trees, blown there by last night's windstorms. He picked it up, his hope restored that she had at least been there for her swim, then kissed it and stored it in his satchel. The next hour, his search was not fruitful. Tears started trickling down his cheeks.

Feeling helpless, he turned his back to the sea and took the return path home.

Back in his neighborhood, he knocked on doors, asking the women if they had seen his daughter, but no one had. When he went to the fourth house, he found the old woman who had known Skylla since her birth in the yard, cleaning fish. She invited him to join her. "You have been rushing around the neighborhood all afternoon. Is everything well with you?" she asked, and stopped scraping scales, resting her knife in the pan.

Phorkys could not hide his distress. He trudged to the chair and ran his hand through his hair. "My daughter has not been back home since yesterday morning. I have not found her. Something terrible must have happened to her." He saw the old woman lift her eyebrows in disbelief. She shook her head.

"That is not like Skylla." Phorkys met her eyes gratefully, and she continued with soothing words. "She is a fine young girl. Something has delayed her, but she will come home." Picking up a red mullet, she started cleaning it and said, "Phorkys, the best place to get the word out and get all eyes looking for her is the agora. You should go there next."

She was right. He went to his house to get a drink, munched on a slice of bread, and headed for the marketplace. He stopped at the usual shops where Skylla liked to shop: the butcher, the baker, and the pottery shop. The owners were all kind, but no one had seen her.

Phorkys spent the next three days asking everyone he came across to keep an eye out for his daughter. One evening, the young lad who had witnessed Skylla being swallowed up in the bay came to his house and told him what he had witnessed. But the old man knew his daughter was a powerful swimmer and found the boy's story hard to believe. He nearly laughed him out of the house. "She could outswim you anytime. Don't spread lies," he scolded him, and bid him goodnight.

With distress in his voice, the young man replied, "I swear not to tell another soul." But it was too late. The news was spreading fast.

The next morning, Phorkys put on his worn himation, for it was windy, and he took the road to the rock for the second time to ask Glaucus for help. The beach was abandoned, the sea rippled with waves. He checked all around the land, then turned toward the rock. Kneeling on the white sand, the old man raised his hands in prayer.

"Kind god, Glaucus, friend of Delos, help me find my daughter, Skylla." He waited for a while, then repeated his plea. Tall waves splashed on the rock, but when the waters settled, the amphibian did not appear. Dejected, Skylla's father shuffled away, feeling the weight of his years crushing on his steps.

That same day, he walked to the sanctuaries to ask Poseidon's priest for advice. "Make a substantial sacrifice, Phorkys," he was counseled, "and soon, before her tracks run cold." The old man returned to his home, sold most of his firewood to his neighbors to raise enough money, and bought a goat from the vendors by the Propylaea.

The next day, he led the animal to the temple. They were ready for him, the priest and maidens, friends of Skylla who trickled in when they heard about the supplication. They gathered and waited for him outside the temple. As the priest sacrificed the animal, spilling its blood on the altar, Aristos's brother, the priest, led with a simple prayer to Poseidon pleading for his help:

Master of the seas, we beseech you,
cast your eyes on Skylla.
Bring her back home.

The chorus of maidens raised their voices, repeating, "Bring her back home . . . back home." They sang hymns on behalf of the community, praised Skylla's virtues, and appealed to Poseidon—who had fathered two daughters—to grant Phorkys his wish. The old man remained kneeling throughout the ceremony next to the priest, repeating every word of his prayers. In his heart, though hurt and upset, he humbled himself to Poseidon, who had taken his son away when the boy drowned in the sea. Wrestling with himself, he had followed the priest's advice to dedicate his heart and his efforts to his living child.

After the sacrifice, alone at home, grief swallowed his heart, his hopes choked. Each morning, a glimmer of hope would ignite fresh energy to search again. He missed her early morning cheer, her greetings, the honey and bread she placed for him on the table before leaving the house for her daily swim. He even missed their quarrels about her escapades in the village square. Her beauty was a magnet for the flirting boys, and he had worried about losing her soon. When he ran into neighbors, they would ask, "Any news yet?" All he could offer in answer was to shake his head.

Each day he would go to the hills to replenish the firewood and avoid their questions. Her absence only encouraged speculation in their community. At the village square and the marketplace, an older woman was heard saying, "She ran away with one of her admirers," with such certainty that many thought it true. Others thought she had drowned. The priest, who knew she was in Messina, kept quiet.

Phorkys's leathered hands ached at the end of the day. He missed the times she filled a basin with warm water for him to soak his hands for relief. His body was exhausted, and yet sleep was elusive. Alone with his thoughts, he would kneel by her bed at night and beg for her safe return, while black holes of fear ate his heart. There were moments of irrational anger, too, for the heartache she caused him. Where was she? What kind of trouble was she in? Didn't she know she was killing him with worry?

The day news reached him about Circe's promise, he praised the goddess and promised another sacrifice once his daughter was back.

TWENTY-SIX

Nightmares visited Circe in her sleep, delivering apocalyptic details. Morpheus was strengthening her resolve to interfere. She became a witness to the horrifying transformation. She watched Glaucus poison the waters just as unsuspecting Skylla swam into his mortifying trap in the deep, dark waters of the bay. A swirl reached out to suck her under the surface.

Circe felt the caustic pain on Skylla's skin. She heard her screams and saw her try to leap out of the water. She felt the wrinkling of her flesh, her hair falling out, her flailing arms, the bulging of her eyes. She squirmed and turned, fighting in her sleep, but the dream would not release her. Six dog heads and twelve feet sprouted out of Skylla's body in an alarming stretch of the flesh. Skylla had turned into a dreadful monster. As the creature attempted to voice her anguish, she let out desperate barks.

The goddess woke up, rubbing her eyes. She pressed her temples to relieve the dread. It was still dark. She had lost her sleep, caught in the concentric circles of a dream that would hold her prisoner.

How could he! How could Glaucus turn young, tall, and limber Skylla into a haunting, ravenous monster? Circe could not forgive him for shifting her flesh, crushing her bones. He had used the enchantress's gift to poison the young woman. Circe paced around the interior of the temple for a while. With first light, she would leave for the strait, but she had to over-come her own fury, for she needed to be light and clear to fly the skies.

Seeking a way to calm her heart, the goddess fell into the simple, elegant ritual her Nana had taught her. The torch that softened the temple's darkness each night was fastened near the altar. She removed it from its bracket and extinguished it in a bowl of water. In the sizzling moment of its death, Circe felt the weight lift from her heart. Dipping a branch of fragrant basil into the water, she sprinkled it around her, chanting incanta-tions that at long last restored her spirit.

Anxious to be on her way, she stepped outside the temple to study the sky, spotting Orion and the Pleiades, and plotted her course to Messina the way Odysseus had taught her. When she saw the first rays of sun rising above the hills, she knew it was time to start on her two-day journey. On a drizzling, chilly morning, Circe left the temple and walked to the top of the hill. There she discarded her leather sandals and tunic, and began to transform, sculpting her body into the familiar shape of a giant bird standing on sinewy legs and powerful talons. The day promised to be sunny and cold. She fluttered her wings, feeling their power, and oriented toward the mainland closest to the Delian coast.

The rising sun found her tearing into the sky, her mighty wings coursing over islands, hills and valleys, and the wintry Aegean, its living waves threatening ships and sailors. In the distance the mainland appeared, a welcome sign of progress. Circe's sharp eyes rested on the craggy lines of Mount Olympus. In an anxious moment she moved higher, letting the thermals carry her off course. She hoped the gods who could see her in the distance would not meddle with her plans.

Back on course, she dismissed her worries. Her eagle eyes surveyed ahead, and she made fast headway over the land and the islands. A few tall-masted ships were crossing the Ionian divide, facing strong winds and the danger of capsizing. Circe maintained her flight above the clouds.

A few hours later, the eastern end of Sicily came into view, reaching to touch the southern tip of a land mass. The narrows were shrouded in fog, almost invisible from a distance. As Circe approached, she dropped lower and saw that for a good stretch the long passage was an arrow's length across. The sound of her flapping wings filled the narrow strip as she entered the rocky cut. She slowed her flight and searched for a perch. She had found the Strait of Messina.

TWENTY—SEVEN

From a lair atop the cliff wall, Skylla's flailing dogs caught sight of a gigantic bird plunging from the clouds and landing on the rocks across. All the dogs knew was hunger and survival. Twelve feet clung to cliff rocks, ready to grab their victims, mostly sailors and large fish, with yelping mouths and gnawing teeth.

The strait was a deadly trap for seafarers who wanted to avoid circumnavigating the island of Sicily. On one side was Charybdis, a large whirlpool capable of dragging a ship underwater; on the other, the monster. Since Skylla's arrival, if seafarers survived Charybdis, the hungry dogs would pick them out and send them to Hades, six at a time. The narrows had turned to a grave.

The landing of the enormous bird surprised the dogs and stopped the ceaseless cooing of pigeons nesting around the narrows, causing the small birds to fly away, startled. Charybdis had no way to drown the visitor. Aggravated, persistent barking reverberated for several minutes, intended to scare the intruder, and six pairs of eyes tracked her every move.

Circe settled calmly and surveyed the narrows. She waited for the barking to stop and then focused on the monster.

First, the sorceress called out to her by name, "Skylla . . ." and waited, but the monster remained still and unresponsive.

She would have to reveal her identity, be more transparent to the girl. Circe moved to shape-shift her upper torso back into her usual human shape to show Skylla who she was. Slowly, her head, neck, bosom, and arms appeared and extended above her wings. This time the monster crawled closer to the ledge, dragging along pebbles and dirt, but made no threatening moves, nor did it bark. Circe called again, "Skylla of Delos . . ."

One prominent dog cocked his head toward the sky, and another looked toward Circe. The two began vocalizing pleas, their yelps dropping into low registers, their eyes sad. The rest of the dogs remained curled up, as if asleep. Skylla must have recognized Circe's upper body, even though it was strange to see the enchantress half-transformed. Circe might have been the monster's first familiar person to come to the strait since Skylla found herself awake in Messina.

Circe flew across the narrows to a rocky perch near the monster's cave. She took her wand out from the folds of her wings and called, "Skylla, I am Circe." The monster did not move.

The sorceress's hands reached for the dog that had made eye contact, and she came cautiously closer. "I am Circe, here to reclaim you," she said in a ringing voice. This time coaxing the monster seemed to work. There was no barking, just a silent recognition in the eyes of all the dogs. Holding her wand firmly in her hand, Circe flew over Skylla and lightly touched the watching dog's head, murmuring incantations. Five more times she touched it, and then withdrew near the cave.

The monster's feet kicked rocks and pebbles that dropped into the water, making a loud splash, and its body began to melt. Layers of unwanted appendages, dogs, and feet peeled off to reveal a beautiful young woman, her body uncoiling, her hair waving in the breeze, her feet unsteady on the ground. She straightened up and looked around. Her eyes revealed fear of the strait. This place where she had stood a murderous guard was baffling and unfamiliar to her human sensibilities. Circe watched Skylla react to the painful energy as she morphed into her human shape.

The enchantress reached out to steady her, and Skylla held on to her arm, pleading with her, "Don't let me go!" The recognition and relief in her eyes were louder than any words.

"Have no fear, Skylla. I am here to free you. This was a bad dream." Circe remained still, letting the girl examine her carefully, fear still lurking in her eyes.

"Circe? Half bird?" Skylla muttered.

The enchantress did not answer. Her energy was focused now on leaving Messina. "I will turn back to a full eagle to take you home. We are two days away from Delos, Skylla," she said with a reassuring smile. It was not a time for lengthy explanations, as the weather was turning and daylight would soon be gone. Winter's dampness had settled over the strait. What mattered most was to get away from this place, to begin their flight.

The enchantress gently waved her wand and dressed Skylla in a white basic tunic and a heavy blue himation with a hood, to keep her warm on the journey. Noticing the girl's puzzled look, she smiled and wondered if she had been aware that she had been bare.

She folded her upper body into fluffed feathers and stretched her neck into a bird's head and beak, assuming her formidable traveling shape. She allowed her companion to watch her, amused by her wide-eyed expression of surprise. Then Circe lowered her body and called to Skylla to climb and settle on her back. She felt the girl straddle her and lean close to her soft feathers, wrapping her arms tightly around her neck. The enchantress rose, moved close to the ledge, and pushed into the wind, her wings flapping fast. Charybdis swirled angrily, as if upset by the loss of her ally. The bird and the girl lifted from the rocks and rose above the narrows, into the setting sun.

By the time Circe turned back to check on Skylla, the narrows were already a distant dot. She wondered if the girl remembered anything from her last moments in Delos. When the enchantress zeroed in on her thoughts, she found Skylla reliving the moment she was getting swallowed by the water; with a grimace of pain, the girl blacked out.

Gradually, Circe realized Skylla's mental state. The girl's recent days as Messina's monster remained locked outside her awareness. Living inside the monster, she had lost a will of her own and was oblivious to her hideous shape and deadly pairing with Charybdis. During this time gap, she had turned into a formidable cannibal who knew not what she was doing. And then, in the rescue, too much had happened so quickly that Skylla was disoriented, holding too tightly onto Circe.

I must find a place to let my rider stretch and get some of her questions answered, thought the enchantress.

When the evening sun set and a quarter moon was up in the sky, an enormous bird and a tiny human began gliding down toward a brown speck in the sea. It was an uninhabited island in the Ionian Sea, the first they came across that would host them for the night.

Circe flew over the coastline, checking for a place to land. High sea stacks were strewn along one side of the island, which was lined with rocky cliffs. She gently touched down at the entrance of a pumice stone cave, high on a precipice, and peered inside. The eagle's enormous size did not allow her to enter, but the ledge was wide enough for her to perch and the interior of the cave was fairly level—a safe place for Skylla to rest. Circe folded her feet under her body outside the narrow entrance, keeping the winds out, and waited for Skylla to hop down. Once on terra firma, the girl moved around the cave, startling the bats that flew away disturbed. Skylla ignored them and stretched her limbs, releasing tension. Turning toward the mighty bird, she joined her hands in gratitude. "Thank you for taking me home," she said.

The eagle settled comfortably by the entrance. She was tired, after all the excitement of getting Skylla safely away from Messina. "We'll stay here for the night."

"But I don't know where I am nor where I have been. Can you please tell me, Circe?" the young woman begged.

"You are safe and heading home, dear Skylla. Your father and friends are waiting."

"Tell me where you found me. And what about a bad dream?"

Circe bit her lip. *Why have I talked about a bad dream? Maybe she doesn't know what happened to her.* "I found you on a long, narrow strait. You never called me for help," she answered in a hesitant voice.

"How did I get there? What bad dream?" the girl persisted.

"We'll have time later to talk. I am glad I found you. Now, get some sleep." The enchantress's tone did not allow for more questions.

It was dark and quiet in the cave. Circe understood that Skylla's limbs were sore and her mind remained puzzled. The girl felt the ground with her hands and found a flat spot inside the cave, close to Circe. There she lay, tucked in her himation, and soon fell asleep.

The eagle fluffed her feathers, tucked her head in, and shut her eyes. She considered that merciful gods, perhaps Poseidon, had intervened and gifted Skylla with a memory seal to lock away into oblivion her Messina days. Recent events might never see the light of day, remaining shrouded in a forgiving cloud of amnesia.

Circe hoped the girl would never know she had consumed Odysseus's men, among them sweet Elpinikis. The chill and intensity of the Strait of Messina had not left her. She tried to clear her mind and anticipate Skylla's questions. Yet she had to wonder if any of that monstrous nature of hunger, greed, and destruction would live on inside this girl. Certainly, Fates had already decided Skylla's future. The girl was made of good and evil and shadows unknown to all, even herself. Circe's role was limited, she knew. Restoring her to her family and community is where her intervention would end. The enchantress finally emptied her mind of this nighttime whirlpool of thoughts, sighed, and drifted off to sleep.

TWENTY-EIGHT

When the sun broke out the next morning, it revealed spectacular arches and sea stacks by their overnight perch. Circe stretched her wings and checked on Skylla, who was still asleep. The girl needed the rest. Transformations demand a lot of concentration and energy. It was so for each creature that morphed into another shape, even a goddess. However, for Circe, shifting into a bird was becoming a favorite form. Floating in the magic of the ether, the lightness and freedom brought her a sense of genuine joy. She flapped her wings, thrust forward, and sliced the wind, landing on top of an arch near the cave. Pillars that sank invisible below the surface of the water supported its massive opening. Millennia of sea waves had licked and pounded into the rock to create the scenery. Circe mused that this massive arch was as close to a tangible companion in eternity as she could have had. Today she felt solid and sound and immortal. Undoing the wrong done to a young girl was satisfying. With eagle eyes, she scanned the open seas, a horizon line unencumbered by any movement, and felt peaceful. Still perched on the arch, she let the playful breezes fluff her feathers and waited for the girl to wake up.

Skylla was stirring. The enchantress flew back to the outer edge of the cave, and when the young woman turned toward the light, she coaxed her with, "Good morning."

The girl got up, dusted off her himation, straightened her

hair, and came outside the cave. "I love the open seas. Where you found me was so narrow and rocky."

"There are places in the world you can't get through without protection from the gods. The strait where I found you is one of them. I am glad we are away from the narrows and on our way to your home," Circe answered.

"A strait? Where is it? I don't know how I got there. What I remember is my beach by the rock in Delos." Her eyes searched Circe's. The enchantress saw her waiting for an answer, an explanation, but she remained quiet. Circe read the questions in her mind: *How did my life become so out of control? How did I get to this strait? How long was I there? How did Circe find me?* Skylla sat on the ground, covered her face with her hands, and began to cry.

Startled, Circe exclaimed, "Here, here! Take some deep breaths, Skylla. Look, you are safe." She waited for the girl to regain her composure, wishing there was more she could do.

Skylla bowed her head slowly to accept reassurance without explication. When she dried her eyes with the back of her hand, she sighed, pulled the himation tight about her shoulders, and brought the hood over her hair. With the eagle's sharp hearing, Circe overheard Skylla mutter, "If Father were here, he would explain what happened to me. I will just have to wait until I get home."

She moved closer to the eagle, looking dejected. Circe's heart went out to the girl, yet she believed the best medicine was to get her back home. The thought of Glaucus poisoning the waters, his vengeful anger, and the consequence to Skylla caused the eagle to stand, raise her wings, and let out a series of high-pitched whistling sounds. Skylla stared at her, uncertainty written on her face.

She's so frightened and upset, Circe was thinking. *Maybe some calming herbs and food would help before we resume our travels.*

"We have a long journey. Come, climb on my back. Shall we look for some food?"

At that, Skylla's spirits shifted and energized; she hopped onto the eagle and wrapped her arms around her neck.

"Are you settled? Good. Here we go." Circe thrust herself away from the ledge, steering inland.

At first, she stayed right below the clouds, to map the land. It was a small island, and the terrain was mostly rocky. Then, close to the ground, she searched for vegetation. On the other side of a hill, she spotted a green grove of tall trees. Fruit dotted the trees that hosted flocks of bright yellow, black-winged orioles, some hiding in the foliage, and others feasting on fallen oranges. The eagle landed and Skylla dismounted. The orioles stopped chirping and, in a panic, scrambled hither and yonder. Skylla laughed her crystal-clear laughter, with the lightness of a carefree trickling brook, for the first time since Messina. *That's more like it*, thought Circe.

Then Skylla ran to a tree and reached high for an orange attached to a branch. She removed it with a twist and rolled it between her palms to loosen the skin. Digging in with her fingers, she peeled it fast and put the first segment into her mouth—and then another. She had not eaten natural fruits since her arrival in Messina. She reached with longing for a second orange, ate it slowly, and when she was done, she ran her hands through the grass to clean them. Then she stuffed as many oranges as she could into her pockets.

Circe found mint, the leafy, fragrant herb that had overtaken the ground in the partial shade of a blackberry bush, a perfect remedy for her anxious companion. She stretched, shook and shed her feathers in a noisy, determined motion, and resumed her human form, mostly to assuage her charge's fears. It did not take her long.

She was Circe, the protective witch, Skylla's unexpected

ally. Leaning close to the ground, she stripped a handful of mint leaves and collected some berries to share with Skylla. Then she took time to groom herself. Stopping on the wide swath of a clear puddle she used for a mirror, she braided her hair with blue, yellow, and white ribbons, and attached a pair of sunburst earrings she loved so much. Over her white tunic, she put on a lovely forest-green himation that she belted with a loose burnt-orange leather strip.

She found the girl that looked her over, impressed. Soon they sat together in the orange grove and listened to the orioles that had resumed their twittering feeding frenzy. Skylla twirled around in a burst of energy, taking dance steps, moving in spiraling circles. It was a joyous reaction to her release from confinement in the lair. When Circe saw her, she laughed. Then Skylla ran and wrapped her arms around the goddess's shoulders. "Goddess, how can I thank you?"

Circe patted her on her back. "I promised myself to keep you safe. It took a while to find you because you never tapped or called me. What do you remember of your last time in Delos?" They settled on the grass where the goddess offered her berries, eating a few herself.

Skylla frowned, concentrating. "I was swimming. As usual, Glaucus was nearby. I snubbed him, wishing he would go away, and moved on to deeper waters, but then a cloud of heat surrounded me. It sucked my energy." She shut her eyes, reliving the moments. "My limbs, my will, were paralyzed. A wave engulfed me. I felt helpless. There was no one close by and nothing to hang on to. I was drowning! I felt an excruciating pain. Burning . . ." She flinched at the memory and opened her eyes. "That is all I remember."

"You must not have had time to call me," said Circe mildly. "But did you ever flirt with Glaucus?"

Skylla blushed. "He kissed me once. It was two years ago. I was curious, and I let him."

Just a kiss? Skylla did not know her venomous amphibian. Just as well, Circe thought, but all she said was, "It's too bad he did not come to protect you." Her brazen lie escaped her lips; it was a convenient cover-up.

Skylla brought her hands to her chest. "It happened so fast. I had no time to think. I don't even want to remember all that." A minute later, she asked, "How long have I been gone from Delos, dear Circe?"

"At least a week. It won't be long before you see your father again."

"He must be frantic! I don't know what I did to deserve this," Skylla said.

"Have more berries. We will not have another meal until tomorrow." Circe handed her the fruit and the leaves she had collected. "Here is some mint. It will refresh your breath, and it's good for digestion. Keep them in your pocket. Chew some anytime you feel like it."

There was plenty of daylight left, and they both were eager to return home. "I will turn into an eagle, Skylla. It's time to continue our journey." She moved behind some brush to shape-shift, though she knew Skylla was stealing incredulous peeks as the eagle grew in size, sprouting black-and-white feathers, a bright yellow beak, and strong yellow talons.

TWENTY-NINE

ully metamorphosed, Circe headed toward Skylla in an awkward, bird-rocking gait. The eagle bent low to the ground to assist the mount, and Skylla climbed onto her back and settled on the familiar curve between the eagle's back and neck. In a show of might, the bird spread her wings, tilted her head, and stretched every feather in the extravagant morning light. Beating the air and tucking her legs under her body, Circe was airborne.

Bundled up in her himation with the hood over her head, the girl leaned low and held on tightly. She relaxed her arms as the bird steadily gained altitude, reaching the cloud cover. They were heading for the mainland.

The island fell behind and the wide sea spread ahead of them. A true Delian girl, she had always loved the sea, rarely missed her morning swims, and relished the deep dives, but this time a knot gripped her throat. What if she fell? She would certainly drown. Holding tightly again, Skylla remembered to chew on mint leaves. She was disoriented, surrounded by the foggy blur of massive clouds. She rested her head on Circe's soft plumage and shut her eyes. Soon the slight rhythmic motion of flapping wings lulled her into a restful sleep.

For a good stretch of time, the eagle glided, keeping her wings flat, soaring high above the sea in the quiet skies. She was thinking about her life in Aeaea. In her early years, she had considered herself invincible, impervious, an untouchable goddess who had set out to organize her life, to be self-sufficient. Her days were not unlike those of mortals. Her passion for nature, her exploration and study, had earned her powers the Olympians were jealous and respectful of. Circe wondered what Skylla's passion would turn out to be. She had watched the Olympians meddle in people's lives and found herself in relationships that had given her a taste of intimacy, love, and eros with mortals— all temporary pastimes in the eternity of her days.

A cloud, a murmuration of starlings that had gathered right ahead of her, interrupted her thoughts. She slowed her pace to give them time to move on. The sight of the eagle had caused instant maneuvering, and the flock took a sudden turn away from Circe, recognizing a fearsome predator. She had no interest in harming them.

Skylla stirred, shifted, and sighed. The girl must have been dreaming.

Circe returned to her thoughts. She remembered Odysseus and other lovers. She had learned from each, experienced highs she would have not known otherwise, just as she hit lows. So would Skylla, as she picked up the thread of her days, and she would also make mistakes. Her own infatuation with Glaucus made her feel gullible, and she realized how poorly she had judged him. What upset her most was that he had used her mushrooms to harm the girl, and worse yet, he had dismissed the girl's right to choose her partners. Most times, people recognized their false assumptions and could change course, like the starlings, but Glaucus had not. She did not feel sorry for his punishment. He deserved the torture of the Furies.

That evening, they landed in Pelion. The view of the bay had alerted Circe that they had crossed over the mainland and were approaching the mountain where centaurs roam, creatures that are part horse, part man, known to be savage forest spirits and regular participants in Dionysian gatherings. The eagle had surveyed the mountain and selected a clearing just as the sunset colors were painting the sky orange and red. She chose the glade for the spring water trickling into a brook that bubbled downhill.

As soon as they landed, Skylla ran to the spring and cupped her hands to collect water, sprinkled it on her face and hands, feeling chill and freshness on her skin. She saw Circe was waiting her turn and made room.

The eagle dipped her head and fluffed out her feathers in the water, sending droplets in every direction. Unprepared, Skylla raised her arms akimbo and took a few steps back to wait for the ritual to finish. Undeterred, Circe splashed for a long time, and when she moved away from the spring, her plumage was soft and sparkling. She flew to the branch of a cedar tree and began preening herself.

Skylla collected apples from trees that bordered the clearing, washed them in the spring, and sank her teeth into the fruit. It had been another full day.

Circe folded her wings in and called to her from the branch she had perched on for the night: "You will soon see your friends and your father."

In the tree's hollow, Skylla gathered some dried leaves and grass to make a soft bed and curled up to rest. She thought of home, missing it as if she had been in exile for years. The aroma of early morning hot water and honey, her father lighting the fire in their warm kitchen, his goodnight kisses paraded in her mind. She thought of friends coming to their yard to speak with them, and the joy of rushing to the square to meet her girl-friends and the special boy. Did he miss her?

THIRTY

*I*t was quiet on the mountain. The occasional call of a screech owl pierced the night. Circe roused enough to check on Skylla and saw that she was asleep. The enchantress was dozing when she heard the clippety-clop of hooves. Weary from travel exhaustion, she had forgotten about centaurs and their love of midnight games.

The faint light of the moon was too meager to discern who was advancing toward them, even for the sharp eyes of an eagle. A pair of bulky torsos were moving into the clearing. They followed a path that took them to the spring, near the cedar tree. "I need a drink," one said.

"I am not thirsty. There is plenty of wine, and Dionysus might join us tonight," answered the smaller centaur. Circe watched them without stirring, hoping they would be on their way soon.

"It will be the same old crowd. Some satyrs too. I love their pipes and jokes!" chuckled the larger centaur.

"Look!" The smaller creature had noticed the girl, tucked into the cavity of the cedar tree. He approached Skylla, and his lips parted in a pleased smile.

Eight hooves and two bellies stood over the sleeping girl. The youngster nudged her with a flick of his tail and playfully said, "Won't you come to the party?" Then he knelt down on his front legs to sniff her body. His companion reared up on her hind legs, protesting, "Don't step on her! Careful."

Skylla felt warm snorts on her neck. With her eyes wide open, she turned toward the younger centaur, more curious than frightened. They were enormous creatures. Their glossy blond coats shone in the moonlight. Their torsos revealed a teen stallion and a middle-aged mare. Shuffling a few steps back, they waited for the girl to sit up.

"Don't mind her," said the young centaur, nodding toward the mare. "She came along, but I found you." He pointed his hoof to his chest. His cheeks were rosy, and as he smiled she could see dimples form. The mare had braided cyclamens in her hair, and the young stallion wore a wreath made of sweet grasses and lavender.

Never before had Skylla seen a centaur, let alone been approached by one. She asked, "Are you creatures of the forest?"

The male pivoted toward his companion and snorted, "She doesn't know!" Turning to Skylla, he beat his hooves on the ground impatiently. Then, softening his tone, he urged her, "We are creatures of Pelion. We mean no harm. We worship Dionysus and will celebrate with him tonight. Join us. You won't regret it!"

During her monster phase, Skylla had become decisive and fearless, because of her exposure to the elements and her own cruel acts. The residue was that she had lost her sense of danger, although she recalled rumors about orgies in Pelion forests and Dionysian celebrations. Skylla moved out of the cavity, leaned on the cedar tree, and examined them curiously. The pair were muscular, playful, powerful—true specimens of nature's fabled creatures. The centaurs stepped back, giving her room. The young woman cast about, looking for Circe, who had left her perch and was nowhere to be seen.

When she saw more centaurs showing up, Skylla frowned. They came adorned with wreaths and beads, cheerful and chatty. Was this a gathering place? An older male came closer to Skylla and lifted her himation, peeking underneath, his eyebrows dancing in a tease. The scatter of centaurs laughed and came closer to watch. She took a step away, annoyed.

"I found her," said the youngster. "Leave her be. She is mine." He moved in front of Skylla, defending his claim, and produced short, raspy snorts, pounding his hooves in the dirt, raising clouds of dust.

"You are too young to have a mate. Move over . . ." grunted the mature male, sizing up his opponent. "I stake my claim to the pretty girl."

"He was here first," spoke up the youth's companion, the mare, challenging the intruder.

Caught in the excitement of the pending scuffle, more centaurs came around and formed a circle. They gleefully placed bets on who would be the winner of the contest. "Wrestle for her . . . wrestle!" they shouted. Cries of "May the best win," were heard as they placed their bets.

Furious, the youngster hurried forward, trying to trip his antagonist, but all he accomplished was to irritate him. It was no longer a game. The circle of curious centaurs widened, making more room for the tussle.

Skylla remained still and searched for invisible Circe. *Where is she? Would she abandon me now?* Grounding herself, she dropped to her knees and covered her mouth so as not to breathe the cloud of dust raised by their hooves.

Unrestrained, the two centaurs backed away from each other, preparing to tangle in dangerous holds. They lowered their heads and began their distance run, dropping their arms, aiming to grab their opponent's front legs.

This time a hyper-alert Skylla called out in a taut voice,

"Circe!" Getting no answer, she crouched lower, watchful, breathing faster.

Skylla had lost track of invisible Circe. As the front legs and arms of the two centaurs intertwined and they butted heads, she heard the muttering of incantations and saw the powerful enchantress's magic wand point to the centaurs. Suddenly everything went still. There would not be a winner tonight. Silence fell on the gathering. The only sound was the trickling brook and the screech owl's call. The frozen crowd of centaurs looked like a haunted collection of statues gathered to watch a wrestling match.

Skylla, who was four feet away from the creatures, raised her head and called out again, "Circe, where are you?" She searched the dark landscape, her eyes darting around the shadows. It was impossible to fathom why these creatures were immobile, encased in their own skin in this three-dimensional still life. Were they still alive? She heard a familiar voice from behind. "I am here. They were getting out of hand."

Skylla turned. Seeing the familiar raptor quelled the tension in her chest. With a sigh of relief, she walked up to Circe, leaned in, and momentarily rested her head on the eagle's wing. Puzzled, she asked, "Why don't they move?"

"They will again, once we leave the mountain."

The massive forms of centaurs punctuated the dark clearing in natural postures: a pair chatting, a few watching the fight, one ready to drink water from the spring. "Magic!" Skylla said, awed. "You are so powerful! But the centaurs could erupt again."

"The beach is safe. It's very close. Climb aboard and I will take us there to spend the rest of the night," answered Circe.

Grateful for the offer, the girl quickly settled on the eagle's back. They rose above the tree line and headed toward the beach, near a grove of pines.

THIRTY-ONE

*T*hey landed on an uneven shoreline strewn with rocky bits, shells, and ropes of seaweed. Although they were away from the immediate antics of the centaurs, Skylla's nervous rush was still coursing through her body. She dismounted from the eagle, shivering in the dark and the briny sea air. "It's cold tonight."

The shoreline was reminiscent of the girl's favorite beach on Delos. She searched for an overnight shelter. Traipsing along the edge of the water, the girl discerned a tall shape, three connected walls and a pile of rocks just where the pine trees started. Circe followed her slowly. It was a structure open to the starry sky but protected. Someone had used it, for there was a fire pit, ashes, and remnants of burned wood.

"A fire would be perfect," said Circe, picking up a couple of pine cones. "These would make good kindling."

"Yes, a fire. Rest up. I will collect more," Skylla said enthusiastically. She carefully walked inside the grove and collected more pine cones and fallen branches, which she piled up in a heap. With a good supply gathered, she carried some to the pit, counting on Circe's magic to start a fire.

The enchantress had not planned on revealing so many aspects of her powers to the girl, but out of necessity, she pointed her wand and sent a flare of heat to the kindling, which began to crackle. Circe settled on the rocks to watch the flames build up. Witnessing witchcraft makes some mortals scared, others overwhelmed, while a few remain curious and want to explore "the dark arts." All along the girl, although awed, had taken it in stride. Skylla fed the fire with large branches, and soon the blaze radiated cozy heat and light, its embers glowing, its flames taming the pitch-dark night.

There was plenty to talk about by the bonfire, their last night before landing in Delos. Circe started the conversation. "Your father will be so relieved to see you."

Skylla sat cross-legged on the sand. Her eyes lit up and she leaned in toward the fire, rubbing her hands together. "I miss him; it will be another sleepless night for him. I am so thankful to you, O Circe, for taking me home."

"What about your boyfriend?"

"Father knows about him." Skylla's cheeks turned rosy in the firelight. "He is a capable man. I think my father likes him."

"It won't be long before you see them," Circe reassured her. "So, what is he like?"

The young woman's features softened as she stirred the wood in the fire pit with a sturdy branch. "You met him the day he came with his friend and they hid my clothes. He is funny, gorgeous, and kind."

Circe smiled. *First love.* "Do you see each other often?"

"Every night I can get away, I meet him at the village square by the plane tree. We walk and talk. He is a good listener and minds my wishes. Sometimes we walk to the beach and sit and talk some more. He has given me a golden ring!" Circe could see the yearning in her eyes.

"He is a lucky lad, and I am proud of you, of how you dealt with the centaurs. You will have stories to tell him," she continued affectionately.

Skylla cringed. "All muscle and presumption. I will remember and talk about them for a long time."

The enchantress considered foretelling Skylla's future: her father's passing, the boyfriend's travels, a life of service in the temple of Poseidon, but she thought better of it. Life would unfold, and Skylla was born to experience the journey. Silence fell between them.

The young girl tossed a large log onto the pyre and lay down, curled up, resting her head on her arms. "I am tired."

Circe's voice was soft. "Sleep. I will watch the fire."

When the sun broke over the horizon, it woke Skylla up. There was no evidence of centaurs. Everything was still and peaceful, birds trilling their welcome songs to a new day. The temperature was warmer than usual and the sea calm. Weary from their journey, they took their time, rekindled the fire, and prepared a meal. Circe roasted some crabs Skylla had trapped from the rocky part of the beach.

Skylla gathered blueberries from the bushes. "At home, Father is up and starting a fire."

"If you need more salve for your father's sore joints, gather cedar leaves to make more when you run out."

"Tell me how, Circe. He uses it every morning."

"Chop fresh cedar leaves and boil them in a small pot. Cover them with a bit of olive oil and simmer slowly. Finally, strain and save the mix for your father."

"So simple. Thank you!"

"Once I have you safely home, Aeaea, my dear home, waits for me. It will soon be spring, time to shear the lambs, make yarn, and dye it to sew clothes and weave tapestries. And we will have a newborn baby to raise. What do you look forward to, Skylla?"

"My studies, my boyfriend, and my father's blessing," she answered, and a smile she could not conceal formed on her lips.

"Do you want to have children?" Circe asked.

"Yes, at least one. My love knows how to navigate the sea, and so will our child. Maybe we will build a home closer to the bay, and I will teach my child to swim." She worked at digging meat out of a crab claw. "I want to study at the temples, learn more about the secrets of nature, about herbs. Father has spoken to the priests, and they have agreed to be my teachers. My love wants to travel the seas, transport merchandise as my brother did. For now, I will maintain Father's home, keep up with my studies, and take care of Father."

She finished eating, turned to Circe, and bowed her head in thanks. Then she washed her hands in the cold sea and started putting out the fire. Circe perched high on a tall tree and checked the horizon line to set her compass for Delos.

"When will I see you again?" the young woman asked.

"I will always be available to you, Skylla. Few women have been born with your gifts. Live and learn from the temples and continue your studies. Your future is bright and promising."

As Circe spoke, Skylla felt enveloped by the goddess's protection and blessings, and raised her right hand: "My loyalty is to you forever, Circe. I have seen the magic you have mastered and will study and learn more about nature. Thank you." They bowed, facing each other.

Skylla tossed sand over the embers, and Circe prepared to launch into the blue sky for the last leg of their trip. Skylla thought, *It's time to go home.*

THIRTY-TWO

irce had settled low to the sand, ready to receive her rider, when Skylla said, "My goddess, I have one favor to ask. When we reach Delos, can we land at my swimming beach? It's the last place I remember." She waited for a minute. "I can pick up my days where I left off."

The enchantress considered it. That spot was crucial; no wonder it was calling Skylla back. But what of Glaucus? Was that place a magnet for him too?

"I thought you would want to see your house, your father first," she countered.

"I do, but landing there feels right. Please?"

The young woman had a point. It was a new phase in Skylla's life. Gods had spared her from having to cope with the ugly monster days for now. When something ends, new endeavors begin. It would be a clearing, a link, a time to pick up anew and move into the future. Reluctantly, she agreed, and the young woman climbed onto the eagle, her himation wrapped tightly around her body, hood over her head, legs astride, and arms loose around the bird's neck.

During the pink hours of the morning, they left the land mass behind, speeding to their destination. Circe rode wintry winds that came in gusts, flapping her wings faster, riding the thermals. Traveling through a cloudscape, she stayed the course, tracking the series of Aegean islands, the last islands on her way to Delos.

In the past few days, Glaucus had been coming to the rock and staying there as long as he could tolerate it. He would longingly sit by, drying his fish body in the sun, depriving himself of the cool, nurturing sea. He forced himself to feel the pain of unnatural dryness on his silver scales. It was a masochistic punishment that mimicked a passive self-flagellation. When he could no longer endure it, he would plunge into the waters for relief and return to the remote coral reef or the deserted caldera at the bottom of the sea.

On those occasions when he visited the rock, in moments of weakness he would indulge in conjuring up Skylla's image. He saw her getting ready for her swim and gracefully diving into the bay waters. He even risked ignoring the Olympians' command and imagined taking her into his arms, only to feel the thin air laughing at him. That is when the Furies' taunts got the loudest, for they would never leave him alone.

The day before, Skylla's young man was roaming the beach, anxiously muttering to himself about his lost love. When he saw Glaucus surface by the rock, he ran toward him, asking for help. In a shaky voice, he said, "Dear Glaucus, help me find my love, Skylla. She is nowhere to be found. Please!"

When Glaucus saw him, he expected his request, but the Furies raised their taunts many decibels up: "Hater . . . Vile . . . Wretch . . ." Desperately, he covered his ears, calling out, "Mercy!" and catapulted himself into the deep waters.

The young man's eyes teared up. He kicked the sand and started pacing. Would he ever see her again?

Skylla took to resting her head on Circe's soft shoulder feathers to avoid the view of the sea below that made her nauseous. She was trying to fill in her memory of the hazy days between her last swim and meeting Circe at the Strait of Messina. A queasy feeling overcame her, no matter how hard she strained to recoup something, anything. All she found was an unexplainable blank. How did she get to the strait? What was she doing? How could time have slipped through her fingers unaccounted? How did Circe find her, and why did the sorceress trouble herself to take her back to Delos?

Circe had begun to descend. When the girl noticed a change in altitude, she sat up, scanning the distance for familiar signs. A land mass came into view, surrounded by water. In the port, she saw several boats and trimmers tied up and a few vessels on dry dock. Skylla, who had never seen her island from above, let out peals of laughter. As they closed in, she could clearly see the hill and recognized the Propylaea, busy with supplicants, merchants, and priests. A wide grin of excitement shone on her face.

Further along, the sandy beach marked by the massive rock was deserted. Circe flew a victory lap before landing and finally let Skylla dismount by the pines. The enchantress watched her delirious dance on the dry needles. A satisfied smile lingered on Circe's face. The young woman turned to the sea, raised her arms in the air, exhilarated, and ran to wade, kick, and splash in the water in boundless celebration.

Out of sight, away from the path to the village, Circe shed her feathers and shape-shifted into a youthful, glowing goddess. She rushed to the rock to survey the coastline. There was no sign of Glaucus. What were the chances that he might resurface? She dismissed the thought. The Furies were keeping watch over him, although they did not restrict where he chose to go. She remained in a quandary about what to share with Skylla.

Skylla's reputation had not been tarnished in the village; only the priest might ever suspect that she had been the

monster that sailors dreaded. Word was out that the creature
had devastated Odysseus's men and more crews as they crossed
the strait. Only Poseidon, the Nereids, and the Furies knew the
monster was Skylla. Circe had undone Glaucus's revenge and
hoped the Furies would keep him away from the young woman.
She looked into the deep waters, knowing that life and fortune
always hold a flip side within them.

The familiar scent of pines, the white sand, and the turquoise
sea filled Skylla's senses and enveloped her in a welcome home.
Her heart was open wide, her stride certain, for she knew this
was where she belonged. She turned and approached Circe,
knelt, and looked up at the goddess, feeling a torrent of thanks.
"Dear Circe, you restored my life. My future is open. I don't feel
trapped. Perhaps I will never know about the strait, but I know
what I owe you. I am forever thankful. Will I see you again?"

"Go in peace, Skylla. Take care of yourself, your father, your
boyfriend. Your life is back on track. Your dreams will lead you
back to your path. Who is to know whether we meet again!
Be strong and curious, and continue your studies. Go to your
home."

Skylla got up and bowed again, keeping her eyes on Circe.
It was time to depart. "I am forever grateful." She bowed one
more time, then turned away to take the dusty path to the village. Skipping at first, she broke into a run, flushed with joy at
the thought of seeing her loved ones.

Circe watched her for a short while, reviewing the growth she
had witnessed. Skylla was no longer an innocent girl. An unexpected turn of events had seasoned her, and she carried a new
awareness of life. The return trip to Delos had given the young
woman space to process and grow in compressed time. When
still a monster, she recognized Circe in the eagle that could

free her from Messina and turned into a trusting traveler. There were more dimensions opening than what she knew before. The world from the sky and witnessing Circe's shape-shifting moments and powers unveiled the existence of new forces. Although she would not remember it, she, too, had shifted shapes. After tolerating the challenge of the amorous centaurs, she had built a fire and cared for a goddess on a chilly night near Pelion. A distinct beauty, Skylla had been gifted with premature strength and a thirst for life. So much unravelling to do! Circe could see in her a curious, strong, resilient yet gentle woman who would pursue her dreams and passions, eagerly gaining a better understanding than most. *Living by water will keep her fresh and Mother Nature will be her teacher, giving her more knowledge and wisdom, as it did for me*, she thought as she lifted off the land.

With her gift to Skylla delivered, it was time for Circe to return to her beloved Aeaea.

THIRTY-THREE

*H*elios rode his chariot over the hillside, spreading the pink shadows of a new day, as Circe approached her verdant island. She dragged her wings through the air to slow before landing. The island had been her base, her place of rest and action, in conflict and peace, and she was ready to settle for a while, to refresh.

Awakened by the flapping of wings, her wild creatures came to welcome her. They gathered around her and watched her shape-shift back to her youthful, glowing self, leaving a tall pile of feathers in a heap. She reached out to her favorites, felt their tawny-beige and gray fur, their powerful muscles that twitched with pleasure at her touch. The island was stirring awake, reverberating with the low, content growls of her mountain wolves and the purring of lions.

Circe stretched her limbs and sauntered to the spring, washed her face, then lifted fresh water in her palms and drank. She noticed birds waiting their turn to splash and preen. Some nests were reinhabited, and others were getting constructed on nearby trees by feathered pairs. There was a liveliness to her footsteps as she climbed up the stairs to her palace.

She walked past her bedroom to her weaving room. Everything looked orderly and picked up. Pulling the curtains aside, she noticed that the oak tree had leafed. The day was warming up. She heard the pitter-patter of footsteps, and when she turned, Melis was standing in the doorway with a dust cloth in her hands. Her servant had dyed her graying hair black. "You look younger, Melis! Spring fever, my dear," Circe quipped, "but flattery will get our people nowhere," and covered a smile with her hand, grateful to have a faithful servant managing her affairs, tirelessly tending to the place.

"I get a lot of compliments, my goddess," Melis responded. "Welcome back!"

It really was her people's home, and Melis ran a tight ship. "We take care of each other," Circe said, her voice rich with emotion, and she reached out and held Melis's hand.

Her servant, smiling, reminded her, "Our pregnant mom is getting close to delivering her baby. Her friends pitch in to help, so she can rest."

Circe looked away, thinking of Elpinikis's horrific demise. "Let me know if she needs my help to birth."

"All is well. We have been waiting for your return to prepare for our annual festivities in honor of the Muses, my goddess. It is that time of the year."

Circe longed to relax. With great warmth she said, "My faithful Melis, I need rest and time alone. A lot has happened on this journey. But first, I want to visit the temple. I will need libations to take with me."

Melis walked to the window and pointed out the small wooden platform that had been constructed a year ago, under the far side of the oak tree. It had been swept clean, and someone had set up a pair of benches.

"Our musicians are already rehearsing, my mistress."

Aeaea's musicians, poetesses, and thespians had been practicing for the island's three-day festival dedicated to the performing arts. It was a special time, one the goddess loved and her people anticipated, preparing for it months in advance. The talented women of Aeaea rehearsed and prepared to perform, compete, take part in processions, and earn prizes. Circe would devote a lot of her time to it.

"I will soon set the start day," she said, and moved away from the window. "Bring me some fresh fruit and libations to take to the temple."

Melis returned an obedient smile and left for the kitchen.

In the afternoon, the goddess took the path to the temple. The sky was dappled blue and white, with a cloud shaped like a gliding bird, its wings spread wide. She could not help but grin, glad to be in Aeaea and done with flying for a while. Along the way, clumps of cyclamens were popping their delicate heads, pushing away the dried leaves of winter. She set down her jars of honey and wine and bent down to pick a few, pinning them to her chest.

Turning to enter the shrine, she saw Perse seated on the temple steps. Her mother was her usual bejeweled self. Today's selection was mostly a theme of turquoise belts, necklaces, and bracelets. She was fanning herself with slow, elegant wrist motions, spreading her perfume all around. Circe adjusted her tunic, struck by her mother's poise and beauty. In her mind, she ran through their recent encounters, from her first dream when she believed Perse was endorsing a relationship with Glaucus to the recent instruction to avoid introducing poisons, advice she had not heeded. What did she want this time? "Mother, welcome to Aeaea."

"I see you are soothing the Olympians today."

"It has been quite a journey, and they did not interfere with my actions this time."

"Moreover, they guided you away from a romance that would have failed, daughter." She laughed to herself sardonically. "I was fooled by Glaucus—fooled by your father too. You must know that I would not have married him had I known him as I do now."

Circe flinched, surprised. "He tries. He loves you, Mother."

"No, he just constantly frustrates me, busy with his consorts!" she said with a bitter grin. "I wish I could get his attention."

"Is this about getting a new palace wing?" Circe asked, and sat down next to her mother.

"I misjudged him. He used to listen. It is good that we are both immortal and he has no power over me, or he might turn me into a monster like Glaucus did to Skylla. He has no respect for me anymore. Just ignores me. Except when he needs me."

Circe did not want to get entangled in their differences. She gave her mother a quick hug that Perse returned. The wheels of her mind spun like a gyroscope searching for a way to avoid an exchange that led to blame. However, this was a rare opportunity to connect with Perse. Perhaps she would ask her advice to resolve a dilemma of her own.

"Mother, I am in a quandary. You know about Elpinikis, Odysseus's sailor who was devoured, died in the Strait of Messina? Should I tell the mother of his child?"

Perse turned, her chin dipping down, thoughtful. "Does she expect to see him again?"

"No, he said his goodbyes. Besides, he did not know she was pregnant."

"If you are the only one that knows this, why not spare her? Let her tell her son about his father when he grows up: the brave hero who fought in Troy, his warrior father."

Circe nodded. This was sage advice. "You are right." She was about to move to the altar and deliver the libations when she offered, "Mother, why don't you stay here for a few days? We have a festival coming up. You can relax and join in. You can take part in whatever way you choose."

It was a first, a first time to extend an invitation of hospitality. Perse moved closer, made eye contact, and searched Circe's eyes carefully. "I think I will." She checked again. "I meant to tell you I am sorry about something. Urging you to seek out Glaucus was wrong, but I meant well . . . I have always aspired to see you paired with an immortal. You deserve one who is devoted only to you. Go on . . ." she said, and waved her daughter on toward the temple.

Circe did not move. She gulped. She had not suspected nor expected her mother to disclose her sentiments and had trouble reconciling them with the Perse she thought she knew. Was there a bond between them after all? Had the umbilical cord meant something? A warm sensation of hope traveled through her limbs. Had she misunderstood her? Surprising herself, she turned, touched her mother's arm and spoke, half to herself, "We are fallible, Mother. I learned a lot on this adventure."

Perse looked at her expectantly.

"Most of all, to avoid assumptions and rely on my firsthand observation of people's actions. It's intention that counts."

She was still considering Perse's apology. She approached the altar and ceremoniously mixed the liquids, then drizzled the thickened blend into a silver bowl she kept on-site. Lifting her arms, she visualized Hecate, the goddess of magic and spells, one her mother also revered. The enchantress poured the libations and drank the remaining mix, then returned the bowl to its place. Kneeling before the altar, she bowed her head and remained still for a minute. Her heart was grateful. The goddess had received her silent thanks. It was time to return to her palace.

The two immortals took the path, their arms locked. It was turning into a new day between them, one that had started with a step toward reconciliation.

THIRTY-FOUR

irce spent the early hours of the next day warping her loom for a new tapestry. She was running through the pastiche of recent memories, plotting, threading them into the canvas of her life. The moment's persistent urge was to create what she had experienced last night in her sleep. She had wrestled with the tangles of the past: faces, links, connections, endearments, birth and death, beginnings and ends. It had been an exhausting and rich night in Morpheus's lap. Could she weave that tapestry? It would be for her own great hall!

From the pile of threads, she picked some skeins and felt their texture on her cheek. An interchange of rough and smooth would give her composition substance. She thought about leaving the beginnings and ends of threads hanging loose, a symbol of unfinished stories, yarns unfolding, a recognition about how memories tinge life and tomorrow is unknown. She could express the notion of time in a dappled sky, keeping it as the background of her composition. The colors would be strong, primary in the center, stretching out in veins, bulging out like arteries that feed and sustain.

She would dot her canvas with entities representing the most important figures in her life, spread out in concentric circles. Helios was simple, easy; the brilliant, arrogant yellow-orange rays of the sun would do. He was her proud, appreciative, and busy father. Perse, her queenly mother, rarely sugarcoated her

171

opinions and demands. She watched over her daughter, making sudden appearances, and she cared. Something between them was shifting. Circe had to search for a suitable symbol.

Just as she laced some blue, gray, and off-white skeins on her bench and was about to begin weaving, her mother walked in. The two had not been under the same roof for a night since Circe's move to Aeaea. The enchantress welcomed her mother, still anxious about how things might go between them.

Perse was in a good mood. The fabric of her tunic was a vibrant palette of spring colors. Her face was relaxed, soft, her eyes bright. She wore a necklace thread of early flowers: crocus, narcissus, cyclamen. On her belt was a string of roses. Circe's mother had tossed a light blue himation over her colorful tunic. She danced around her daughter, moving toward the window. "Helios sent a messenger this morning. I am needed at the palace." With a pleased smile, she continued, "Besides, I miss home. I have been away a lot."

Circe swallowed, feeling a pang of guilt for not seeking her out earlier in the morning. "Can we share a meal before you go? Is Father welcoming or upset?"

"Something light. As for your father, I really don't know. He probably needs me to host some event, guests . . . but I will return to attend the opening of your festivities. When do you plan to set it?"

Just then the sound of aulos sweetly pierced the morning. It was coming from the stage, a practice session from an aspiring contestant. Circe smiled to herself, threw a himation over her tunic, and stepped outside. She led the way. "In seven days, Mother. I hope that gives us both time to take care of tasks ahead."

There was a crisp chill in the air, but shafts of light warmed the gazebo outside. Circe cleared dry, fallen leaves from a couple of benches and invited Perse to the table. They continued chatting amicably, enjoying fresh apricots and walnuts. Melis, who tracked her mistress day and night, had quietly served them.

The two women heard the rustle of a pair of cats nearing the table. The animals were approaching Circe, very affectionate, wanting her attention. They rolled on the ground and persisted, demanding neck rubs. Circe indulged and then dismissed them. Leaning back at ease, she reminisced, "I saw little wildlife in Delos. But I remember the poisonous snake that crawled out of the bleached deer skull the day you appeared on the hillside."

Perse leaned closer to Circe and fixed her eyes on her daughter. "I was glad you killed it. I was hoping that you would pay attention to my warning not to share information and samples of poisonous plants with Glaucus."

The enchantress felt heat rising in her face, caught unaware. "Did you send it? As a message?"

"Yes. By then, I knew his feelings and intentions about Skylla were dangerous."

Circe gulped, astonished. "I missed it, Mother!"

In a soft voice, Perse answered, "I realized later you did, my dear, when I saw you giving him the mushrooms." Circe ran their exchange on the hill through her mind. Could it be that she had misunderstood her mother's desire to support her? Could it be that her mother was a laconic, sometimes gruff, but well-meaning, restless woman?

As if indifferent, Perse turned her attention to a couple of sparrows that argued over fallen walnuts and tossed a few more to the ground. She watched them and laughed. "Look at this pair. They are fighting over one walnut, but there are more to pick right here! So it is with men. No rush, plenty to pick from." Laughing, she got up and turned away.

Circe was intrigued. "So much more to talk about, Mother! I will await your return."

Perse moved a few feet away from the gazebo, and just before she was out of range she affirmed, "I will be back. You are my special daughter, my dear. But it's time to leave you for a while."

Circe barely had time to breathe another word. "Soon, Mother . . ."

Perse turned toward the wind and faded from view.

GLOSSARY

GODS

AEETES: Son of Helios and Perse, Circe and Pacifae's brother. He is a sorcerer who reigns in the Kingdom of Colchis. His name comes from the ancient Greek word that means "eagle."

AEOLUS: The god of winds, he appears in Homer's *Odyssey*, giving Odysseus a bag containing storm winds to keep, protecting him from danger. Unfortunately, greedy companions open the bag looking for gold, and the winds lead the ship back to Aeolus's island.

APOLLO: Son of Zeus and Leto, Apollo is one of the twelve gods of Mount Olympus, the god of music, poetry, light, prophecy, and medicine. He was born and worshipped on the island of Delos, where mortals build him a magnificent temple.

ATHENA: Athena, one of the twelve gods of Mount Olympus, is the goddess of battle strategy and wisdom. She is always accompanied by her owl and is the goddess of victory. Odysseus is a mortal under her protection.

CIRCE: Ancient Greek goddess, an enchantress and a minor goddess in Greek mythology. She is the daughter of the god Helios and the Oceanid nymph Perse. Circe is renowned for her vast knowledge of potions and herbs. In Homer's *Odyssey*, she changes a band of Odysseus's men into pigs, takes Odysseus as a lover, and eventually aids them as they depart for their home in Ithaca.

CYBELE: Great Mother of the Gods, predominant in Greek literature. She is the mistress of wild nature (symbolized by her constant companion, the lion), a healer, the goddess of fertility and protectress in time of war.

DEMETER: She is the Olympian goddess of harvest and agriculture, presiding over grains and the fertility of the earth. When Hades, the brother of Zeus and god of the underworld, abducts her daughter, Demeter goes in search of her daughter. When she cannot find her, she refuses to let anything grow. The final compromise is to release her daughter to her mother half the year and keep her in Hades the other half. When Demeter has her daughter, nature flourishes in spring and summer, giving crops and brightness to people.

ERATO: One of the fifty daughters of Nereus (eldest son of Pontus, personification of the sea) and Doris (daughter of Oceanus, a Nereid), whose name means "the Lovely."

GLAUCUS: In Greek mythology, Glaucus is a Greek prophetic sea-god, born mortal and turned immortal upon eating a magical herb. It was believed that he came to the rescue of sailors and fishermen in storms, having earlier earned a living from the sea himself.

HECATE: Hecate is the chief goddess presiding over magic and spells. She witnessed the abduction of Persephone, Demeter's daughter, to the underworld and, torch in hand, assisted in the search for her.

HELIOS: Helios (also Hellios) is the god of the sun in Greek mythology. He was thought to ride a golden chariot that brought the sun across the skies each day from the east to the west. He is married to Perse and is Circe and Aeetes's father.

HEPHAESTUS: He is the crippled son of Zeus and Hera, famous for his skills for smithing weapons for the gods, and protector of blacksmiths, sculptors, and fire.

MOPHEUS: Morpheus is one of the sons of Hypnos (Somnus), the god of sleep. Morpheus sends human images (Greek morphai) of all kinds to the dreamer, while his brothers send forms of animals and inanimate things, respectively

NEREIDS: Fifty sea nymphs, daughters of Nereus and the Oceanid Doris, frequent companions to Poseidon, god of the sea.

PENELOPE: She is a character in Homer's *Odyssey*, the queen of Ithaca, the daughter of Spartan king Icarius and naiad Periboea. Penelope is known for her fidelity to her husband Odysseus despite the attention of several suitors during his absence.

PERSE: In Greek mythology, Perse is an Oceanid nymph, and one of Helios's three wives. She is the mother of Circe, Aeetes, and Pacifae.

POSEIDON: Poseidon, one of the twelve gods of Olympus, is the god of the sea (and of water generally), earthquakes, dolphins, and horses.

RIVER STYX: It is the principal river that separates the world of the living from Hades, circling the underworld seven times, thus separating it from the land of the living.

ZEUS: He is the sky and thunder god in ancient Greek religion. He rules as king of the gods of Mount Olympus. His symbols are the thunderbolt, eagles, bulls, and oak trees.

MORTALS AND MORE

AEAEA: It is a mythological island said to be the home of the goddess-sorceress Circe, on the Eastern Mediterranean, according to classical Greek scholar Dr. Ioannis Kakridis.

ARISTOS: A fishmonger who lives on the island of Delos and offers helpful information to Circe about Delos. The character was constructed to play his part in this novella.

CHARYBDIS: She is believed to be a large whirlpool capable of dragging a ship underwater and a sea force that lived on one side of a narrow channel opposite Skylla. Sailors crossing the narrows attempting to avoid one of them would come in reach of the other. The expression "between Skylla and Charybdis" means to be presented with two opposite dangers; the challenge is to find a route that avoids both.

DELOS: A Greek island on the Aegean Sea that was both an influential political force and, with a sanctuary dedicated to Apollo, an important religious center during the Archaic and Classical periods. The island was also a major commercial and trading center.

ELPINIKIS: A trusted sailor from the island of Ithaca who travels with Odysseus and lives on Circe's island, Aeaea. The character was constructed to play his part in this novella.

HIMATION: An outer garment worn by the ancient Greeks over the left shoulder and under the right.

HIPPOCRATES: An ancient Greek physician traditionally referred to as the "Father of Medicine" in recognition of his lasting contributions to the field. Today, new physicians take the oath named after him, to uphold professional and ethical standards.

MELIS: Circe's trusted head servant who manages the women living and serving on the island of Aeaea. The character was constructed to play her part in this novella.

MESSINA: The Strait of Messina is said to be where the sea-monster, Skylla, and Charybdis waited for ships and sailors to devour. It is a narrow strait between the eastern tip of Sicily (Punta del Faro) and the western tip of Calabria (Punta Pezzo) in Southern Italy.

NANA: Circe's governess, a mortal priestess chosen by Perse and charged with the goddess's upbringing. The character was constructed to play her part in this novella.

ODYSSEUS: He is a legendary character, king of the island of Ithaca, who fought in the Trojan War. He is known for his intellect and cunning. Homer tells of his adventures of returning home after the end of the Trojan War in the *Odyssey*. He lives on Circe's island for a year before departing for his home in Ithaca.

ORION: A constellation visible throughout the world, named after a hunter in Greek mythology, used by sailors for navigation.

PLEIADES: Also known as the seven sisters, protectress of sailors, daughters of Atlas. It is a celestial cluster used for navigation.

SKYLLA: Skylla is a sea-monster who haunted the rocks of a narrow strait opposite the whirlpool of Charybdis. Ships that sailed too close to her rocks of the Strait of Messina, between Sicily and Italy, would lose sailors to her ravenous, darting heads.

SOPHOCLES'S *ANTIGONE*: Sophocles is an ancient Greek author of tragedies. *Antigone* is one of his three Theban plays. The chorus delivers the famous line "Ἔρως ἀνίκατε μάχαν," expressing how defenseless people are in eros's presence.

THESPIAN: An actor. The word is related to Thespis, the man who first took the stage in Ancient Greece. As an adjective, the word *thespian* describes someone who is related to drama.

TIRESIAS: In Greek mythology, Tiresias was a blind prophet of Apollo in Thebes, famous for his clairvoyance.

TROY: City at the entrance to the Hellespont and the center of Priam's kingdom. Homer's *Iliad* and *The Odyssey* are epics about the Trojan War. Troy is destroyed at the end of the war.

PHORKYS: According to Acusilaus, he is Skylla's father. In mythology, there are several names attributed to Skylla's father, all associated with the sea.

ACKNOWLEDGMENTS

*T*his novella would not have been possible without the support and encouragement of so many lovely people. I particularly want to thank the Women of a Certain Age (WOACA), Diana English, Lisa Graham-Peterson, Meg Mahoney, Christine Noelle, and Mary Weikert for being part of early reviews, drafts, and redrafts of the English version. Efi Metaxa has been my tireless beta reader of my draft translations of this book into Greek.

Generous editorial guidance came from Susan Meyers and Jean Gilbertson, Seattle area professionals. Their easy availability and thoughtful feedback were exceptional.

Much of my preparation for this project came from author groups and classes. I want to express my appreciation to my current and past teachers, Brenda Peterson and the Salish Sea Writers, Theo Nestor, Susan Meyers, Scott Driscoll, and several other Hugo House instructors who helped me level up and stick to completing this project.

I am indebted to She Writes Press (SWP), especially to Brooke Warner and Shannon Green, who shepherded this book into the world, as well as Christine Collenette, CEO of Surpassem, Cristina Deptula, Seattle She Writes Press writers, and my 2021 SWP cohort, who have done more than I ever could to market, promote, and share ideas and support all along.

Finally, I am grateful to my grandsons, Oscar and Damon, who are fond of their Greek heritage and have enjoyed reading stories with ancient Greek heroes and heroines. That has made my work so much more fun and meaningful.

ABOUT THE AUTHOR

Sophia Kouidou-Giles was born in Thessaloniki, Greece, and university-educated in the USA. She holds a bachelor's degree in psychology and a master's in social work. In her over-thirty-year child welfare career, she served as a practitioner, educator, researcher, and administrator and published articles in Greek and English professional journals. In recent years, her focus has shifted to writing nonfiction, fiction, poetry, and translation. Her work has appeared in *Voices, Persimmon Tree, Assay, The Raven's Perch,* and *The Blue Nib.* Her poetry chapbook is *Transitions and Passages.* Her work has appeared in anthologies, including *The Time Collection, Visual Verse,* and *Art in the Time of Unbearable Crisis.* Her memoir, Επιστροφή Στη Θεσσαλονίκη/*Return to Thessaloniki,* was published in Greek by Tyrfi Press. *Sophia's Return: Uncovering My Mother's Past* is published in English by She Writes Press. *Perse,* the sequel to *An Unexpected Ally,* will publish in November 2025.

The author lives in Seattle, Washington, near her son, daughter-in-law, and two grandsons. You can find more about Sophia at www.sophiakouidougiles.com and www.facebook.com /sophiakg.

SELECTED TITLES FROM SHE WRITES PRESS

She Writes Press is an independent publishing company
founded to serve women writers everywhere.
Visit us at www.shewritespress.com.

Bridge of the Gods by Diane Rios. $16.95, 978-1-63152-244-4. When twelve year-old Chloe Ashton is abducted and sold to vagabonds, she is taken deep into the Oregon woods, where she learns that the old legends are true: animals can talk, mountains do think, and deep in the forests, the trees still practice their old ways.

Return of the Evening Star by Diane Rios. $16.95, 978-1-63152-545-2. In this second installment of the Silver Mountain Series, Chloe Ashton and her friends race to protect the people and animals of Fairfax, who have come under attack from speeding ambulances that prowl the land, mowing down anything in their path and dragging their victims to a mysterious hospital deep in the woods.

Trinity Stones: The Angelorum Twelve Chronicles by LG O'Connor. $16.95, 978-1-938314-84-1. On her 27th birthday, New York investment banker Cara Collins learns that she is one of twelve chosen ones prophesied to lead a final battle between the forces of good and evil.

Gravity is Heartless: The Heartless Series, Book One by Sarah Lahey. $16.95, 978-1-63152-872-9. Earth, 2050. Quinn Buyers is a climate scientist who'd rather be studying the clouds than getting ready for her wedding day. But when an unexpected tragedy causes her to lose everything, including her famous scientist mother, she embarks upon a quest for answers that takes her across the globe—and uncovers friends, loss, and love in the most unexpected of places along the way.

Moon Water by Pam Webber. $16.95, 978-1-63152-675-6. Nettie, a gritty sixteen-year-old, is already reeling from a series of sucker punches when an old medicine woman for the Monacan Indians gives her a cryptic message about a coming darkness: a blood moon whose veiled danger threatens Nettie and those she loves. To survive, Nettie and her best friend, Win, will have to scour the perilous mountains for Nature's ancient but perfect elements and build a mysterious dreamcatcher.

Provectus by M. L. Stover. $16.95, 978-1-63152-115-7. A science-based thriller that explores the potential effects of climate change on human evolution, *Provectus* asks a compelling question: What if human beings were on the endangered species list—were, in fact, living right alongside our replacements—but didn't know it yet?